Spring, summer and fall: Blackwater Press 2001

Mamie Cadden, backstreet abortionist: Mercier Press 2003

St Audoen's National School 1756-2006: The Board of management 2008

Acknowledgements
I am grateful for the technical and artistic assistance I received from Trevor J Noble.

I also acknowledge the encouragement I received from the the Public Record Office at Kew.

This book is dedicated to the memory of Tom Kavanagh(1903-1992), grandnephew of Crimee Tommy.

Crimee Tommy

Ray Kavanagh

Published by Ray Kavanagh 2024
Copyright Ray Kavanagh 2024

Also available as an Amazon ebook

ISBN 9798344101828

Contents

Chapter 1 The night of the big wind	1
Chapter 2 A famine wedding	25
Chapter 3 Crimee Tommy	56
Chapter 4 Into the Crimea	85
Chapter 5 Outside Sevastopol	106
Chapter 6 Into the valley of death	122
Chapter 7 When the battle's done	137
Chapter 8 The day has come	162
Chapter 9 The green flag of Erin	182
Chapter 10 The prodigal son	203
Chapter 11 Sweet Avondale	236
Chapter 12 A thief in the night	254

Chapter 1

The night of the big wind.

6th January 1839.

The pains started when she was drawing water from the well. It was stupid wasn't it drawing water at this time of the day especially as the wind was howling so? What kind of night would it be with the wind breezing so high that she was nearly lifted out of it on her way? There was going to be a great storm alright. But she would still get a half-bucket of water home; it would hold her down on the road back. She'd need it for sure when the baby came.

Back in the house her 19 year old husband Willy was sitting there staring into the fire, handsome as the day she married him. He was bent over on his three-legged stool with his elbows resting on his thighs, he looked as if he was asleep with his eyes open, all in a world of his own. On the other side of the fire was his old mother Annie, grey haired and smiling at nothing with her hands clasped under her stomach. She was doting now and had been for a year or so but harmless and no worry at all. She was more like a baby than an adult but Catherine didn't mind her, in fact she was fond of the old woman, there was many a wife that had an ould bitch of a mother-in-law and she was grateful that Annie was such quiet old woman, friendly and helpful before she went into her dotage and now she was no trouble at all. Anyway Willy was very close to her and when you took a husband you took on his whole family too.

That's the way of the world, she thought and not a bad thing either. She might be in the same position as the old girl herself some day and it would be nice to be treated with kindness.

The house was full of smoke now as the down draught caused by the wind filled the one-roomed cabin but it didn't bother the two sitting at the fire, they were used to it.

Catherine left the half-bucket of water on the mud floor just inside the door. "The pains have started Willy" she said, "The babby's coming, go and get Mrs. Delaney". His eyes opened wide "Will you be alright on your own your with Mammy?" he asked. He stood up and shook himself. "Don't be annoying me now, go and get Mrs. Delaney, I'll need her soon, I'm going to lie down. Be as fast as you can, tell her it won't be long." "I've tied down the roof good and tight, there's a fierce storm coming up." "Willy, go and get Mrs. Delaney" said Catherine as she untied her pinafore and hung it over the single chair in the room. She was a small shapely woman with her chestnut brown hair which was admired so much, and tied back with a red ribbon. She then went over and squeezed her mother-in-law's hands for good luck. Old Annie stared at her with glazed, rheumy, confused eyes and her head nodding constantly as it had done for these past few years but she smiled beautifully at her daughter-in-law.

Willy was a good man but a bit too easy going especially when there was a hurry on like now. Ah! but she was lucky to have such a decent man, many's a girl had a drunkard for a husband or a man that would bate them, more fool they, if any man laid a hand on her she would give them something to think about. Willy was as gentle as a lamb and a great provider, neither she nor the babby would go hungry while Willy was around. He worked as a yardman on the O'Reilly estate as had his father before him.

The Brennnans had come down from Dublin with the O'Reillys about fifty years ago when they had bought the estate in old King George's time. Today Willy had been sent home from the Yard. No work could be done because of the impending storm. The animals were housed safely and nothing was left lying around. That was all that could to be done, then everyone was sent inside and sit out the tempest. Willy, Catherine and his mother lived near the small village of Kildangan in south of county Kildare in a townland called Killeen, situated in the east of Ireland. It was rich farming land. To the north of the county was the rolling plain of the Curragh which housed a huge military camp. There was little else in the county; farmers, soldiers and the tradesmen in the towns. It was a prosperous and peaceful place.

Catherine shushed the hens off the bed in the corner and unloosened her dress. She eased herself gently onto the bed. "Please God and his blessed mother that the child won't come before Mrs. Delaney arrives. I wouldn't know what to do" she muttered to herself. It was to be her first child. "And please God the babby will be strong and healthy like his Mammy and Daddy" and then she said out loud "Why shouldn't he be?" She had a habit of talking to herself when she was alone. She said a Hail Mary quietly to herself begging the Virgin for a safe delivery and a healthy child.

Meanwhile the winds howled outside. All the countryside had emptied and was gone indoors save for a few solitary stragglers out on a mission like Willy Brennan or those so stupid as to ignore the signs of nature that foretold of a wild storm to come. The birds had disappeared hours ago, sensing the danger in the air and all the poultry, pigs and other livestock had been taken indoors. Their pig was safely locked up with their cow. He despised the lazy folk who kept a pig in their own kitchen, so backward and dirty. Besides the howling gale, the only sound to be heard was the yelping of the few terrified dogs that had been cruelly left tethered out of doors by their inconsiderate and cruel masters.

Their howling was a horrid and frightening sound, the sound of terror. The dogs sensed the oncoming storm and wanted to shelter or run from it. All the animals knew what was coming. Their instinct was a wonderful thing, far better than that of the humans they served. Willy struggled against the gusts and towards Mrs Delaney's cabin. The wind was stronger now and seemed to be rising all the time. Sometimes he was nearly lifted off the roadway as if he were no weight at all against the power of the wind but he struggled on bareheaded and afraid of the gusts belting into him. He was thrown around the road time and again and fell three times, struggling to get up and push himself on. But there was no question of giving up and turning back.

Catherine depended on him and the new baby too. He hoped to God that Mrs Delaney would not be too terrified to venture out on such a day. She was a kind old woman, a widow herself who kept body and soul together by helping at the birth of the children for the people of Kildangan and the few coppers or an apronful of spuds or a few eggs they would give her in return. She was also the best laugh of all the old women around here and had the dirtiest mind. He loved her company. But she was also a very skilled woman, his own mother used to swear by her saying that she had a gift of helping at a delivery and that it was bad luck or downright meanness not to use the good little woman. It was Mrs. Delaney's proud boast that she had help deliver three generations of Kildangan children. In spite of the raging storm he knew that she wouldn't let them down, hadn't she been present at his own birth and that of all his family?

She lived in a one room cabin, just off the road and about a mile from his own place and just after the row of cabins that passed for the village of Kildangan. Her house was lower than the others and in poor shape. It had just one window, which was now boarded up

against the howling wind, and even though he knew he could walk straight in he still belted on the door.
"Are you there Mrs. Delaney?" he shouted against the howling wind. "Come in if you're good looking" she cackled loudly in response almost as if she had been waiting for him.

"Ah, its you Willy" she said as he entered as if she didn't know him already by his voice. He pushed the door closed and replaced the latch against the tempest outside. The old lady sat on a three-legged stool by the fireside though there was no fire in the grate. The room was dark and he could barely make her out except for her shape. "What are you looking for? As if I don't know, you men are always only looking for the one thing, well ye might be in luck, ye dirty little rascal." "Stop that oul talk now Mrs. Delaney" Willy replied. "Catherine's time has come and she needs you." "Ye didn't time that very well, did ye? Could ye not have done it week before and it would have been all over and done with by now? This is no day to bring a babby into the world"

"There's an awful storm outside, I wouldn't be too sure of your roof before the night is out, could you not have getting someone to tie it down for you?" he asked. "Sure who would I have to ask except yourself, a poor widow woman like me?" "Anyone of the neighbours would have done it for you" he replied "Sure they don't have enough wit to do it for themselves. When did the pains start anyway?" she rejoined as she put her shawl over her shoulders.

"She went out to the well for a bucket of water awhile ago and when she came back she was complaining." "I'll get my bottle and come along directly, mind you'll have to take a good howt of me on the road or I'll blow away in that storm, a frail little creature like myself." "I'll hold onto you" Willy said, knowing full well what was coming next. "Good be God" she said "I didn't have a good howlt in ages" The two of them left the little house laughing and headed out into the howling winds. "Mother of God" she said when the gusts hit her, "It must be the end of the world."

He clutched her tightly as they moved down the road and she nestled into the shape of his body. "She must have been a right little fine thing in her day," he thought and as if to echo what was in his head she shouted into his ear "If I was twenty years younger we'd be heading into that ditch for a bit." "Go away out of that Mrs." He shouted into her ear. He wouldn't admit it to her it that it had crossed his mind too. "An oul wan like you should be saying her prayers and leave that sort of stuff to the young people." "If I was praying I know what I'd be praying for. He knew he would only encourage her banter if he replied to this, anyway he was feeling a little bit frightened of the wind at this stage. It could do them an injury if it lifted them off the road and hurled them down against it, especially an old woman like Mrs Delaney. He held her tightly now as the wind whipped against them raising her skirts and buffeting them from one side of the road to the other. He'd never forget this day, he thought. Not a soul to be seen around Kildangan.

Even the local layabouts had moved indoors for the first time in their lives. It looked like a dead place without even a few fowl scratching around. Anything unsecured was blowing madly around the street and he could see the thatch lifting from some of the houses. They'll regret their laziness in not tying down their roofs in the morning or even in the middle of the night when the whole lot lifts off and sails away as far as Monasterevin or even farther and they'd be exposed to the elements as much as any beggar man and his family.The thought gave him satisfaction as his own cosy little house came into his mind with the little outhouse at the side. He had spent hours that morning tying down the roof with the straw ropes and burying them into the ground then covering them with rocks and scraws. He pulled the warm body of Mrs. Delaney even closer and thought of his own Catherine lying on the bed waiting for their first child and cursing him for taking so long. She was a lovely girl and so full of spirit. He loved when she chided him; she was just like his own mother before her dotage. What more could a man ask for?

Soon his own cottage came into view and it was taking a battering from the wind. Now stinging rain mixed with the howling gale as he dragged Mrs. Delaney towards the door.
He wished his own mother had her wits about her and was able to supervise and advise and boss everyone around. But she was doting now and was as helpless as a child. Ah sure that was the way of the old people if

they lived that long. Though he had confidence in Mrs. Delaney he wished for the reassurance his own mother would provide. She would be thinking of him from the small part of her mind that wasn't confused. What if something went wrong? Many women died in childbirth in these parts, especially for those having their first baby. It was a dangerous business.

But Catherine was a strong and brave girl and Mrs Delaney a great midwife. Inside the house, the midwife took immediate charge as if it were her own place. Catherine lay moaning on the bed just giving him a pained smile when they walked in. "You took your time" she moaned.
"You look after the fire and heat up some water" Mrs Delaney ordered. "And keep your eyes to yourself, it's not fitting for a man to be prying around at a birth, its women's business"
Willy retreated to the fireside and sat on the three-legged stool beside his mother who seemed oblivious to the presence of the midwife.

"You shouldn't be here Willy son" she said echoing Mrs. Delaney's words. Sometimes she was lucid and clear headed."It's alright Mammy," Willy replied softly "There's a storm raging and I can't go outside"
Needlessly he started to poke the smouldering embers in the fire. Gusts of smoke from the chimney filled the already smoky room. He could hardly see Mrs Delaney though she was just a few feet away at the bedside .He didn't need any instruction not to watch. He was mortally embarrassed anyway and if it wasn't for the

storm he'd have gone outside to walk around until it was all over or he was called for. Or gone to Jimmy Kennedy's shebeen in the village and gotten drunk like some of the men did by custom, there would be plenty of company there today but he wouldn't do that to Catherine, not today anyway, maybe after the babby was born. He lifted the kettle off the crane and ladled it half full with water from the bucket that Catherine had taken in from the well. He returned it to the crane and pushed it over the half-dead fire which he stoked and to which he added a few sods of turf.

Mrs Delaney took Catherine Brennan in her arms and soothingly said "Hush alanna, it'll be fine in awhile, its only the little babby trying to get out, sure he's feeling it a tight pinch inside a little creature like you, We'll have you right as rain in awhile".

Catherine allowed herself a little laugh at the idea a baby inside her trying to get out and immediately felt better.   Then the pains started again and worse this time. "Kneel up on your hunkers darling" said Mrs. Delaney "and I'll give you a little wash, that'll make baby come out easier." "Willy" she said "Bring over a bowl of hot water, not scalding mind" "How can I do that without looking?" Willy answered sheepishly. "Oh God deliver us from men this day" Mrs. Delaney replied as she got to her feet and went over to the fire. "Can you get me a bowl to put the water in at least?" she demanded of the unfortunate husband as he crouched by the fireside.

He got up and took the three-legged iron pot from the

table that they used for the potatoes and handed it to the midwife. Mrs Delaney wiped it out with her apron and half filled it with water from the bucket and topped it up with hot water from the kettle from the crane. She then returned to Catherine who was kneeling up in the bed. Her face was contorted with pain and Mrs Delaney pulled up her dress and removing a rag from her sleeve started to wash and massage her charge, rubbing her swollen belly with the damp warm cloth. After the washing she rubbed in some goose grease which smelled a bit but was great stuff, she swore by it for easing a delivery and never went on a call without a bottle of it. "It won't be long now darling," she said as she wiped Catherine's face with the rag. Her face was streaming with tears of pain and anger. "My God" she thought "I'm going to die with the pain, is there no end to it?

But she said nothing, just waited as the throbbing continued. "I wish my Mammy was here, Mrs Delaney" moaned Catherine. "Yer Mammy's in heaven praying for you this day, she'll make sure everything's alright for you, don't you fret". As if reminded of divine intervention in the affair she called over her shoulder to Willy "Get me a drop of Holy Water will you?" Willy shuffled over with an uncorked bottle, which Mrs. Delaney sprinkled, on the mother-to-be.
"Pray to yer Mammy now she'll ask the Virgin to look after you".

Susan O'Reilly aged 12,
heiress to Kildangan House and estate.

Part II

Standing at the window in Kildangan House was a small brown haired girl of twelve years. The mansion was the property of Captain Dominick O'Reilly RN as was the village of Kildangan and all the lands thereabouts. The young girl was staring into the gathering darkness and fascinated by the rising storm. This was Susan O'Reilly, the daughter of the house and the only surviving child of the Captain. She had been told more than once to come away from the window but Susan was fascinated by the winds. She had never witnessed anything like it before. It seemed if the whole country was being blown around. She could even feel the thatch on the roof moving. Unusually for a landlord's house it was thatched. Captain O'Reilly had refused to have it replaced by slates as most of his neighbours had. To mortgage his estates for the sake of fashion was the height of foolishness he thought and anyway he liked the thatch. It was warm and colourful. The big sash windows in the house were rattling though. But she wasn't afraid, her Papa had told her never to be afraid and he always knew what to do. He was the bravest man in the Queen's Navy and she would do anything for him. He looked just like Lord Nelson in his uniform and every bit as proud but of course he had both arms and eyes unlike the hero.

She wished he was here tonight and every night but he would be when he left the Navy and returned home. Oh! how lovely that would be, the family together again.

Maybe Mama and Papa would have more children: another girl would be nice for company and to play with, it was lonely having no brothers or sisters and sad to think of her poor dead brother Dominick and her two dead sisters but Papa had told her to be brave and she would. Mrs. O'Brien was a right old fusspot trying to get her away from the window on a night like tonight, the best night of the year, well maybe not better than Christmas or when Papa was home but a great sight all the same. She was still on her Christmas holidays from school and loved being at home though she also loved the gentle and holy nuns of the Loretta Order and especially all the other girls in their school in Dublin. She hoped the workmen and the tenants were safe in their little houses but Mrs. O'Brien said it was nothing for her to worry her pretty head about. All the same she didn't think some of their little houses would withstand the storm. "Sure can't they build them up again in no time," her nurse had replied with a kindly smile on her face.

She always had an answer had Mrs O'Brien but she had gotten really annoyed at Susan's insistence at standing at the window to look out at the storm. "Its no place for a young lady to be seen, looking out a window like a serving girl" the old woman had insisted. "But Mrs O'Brien nobody could possibly see me, there is no one out tonight in the storm, they'd be blown away!" smiled Susan sweetly. Her nurse, a short plump woman in her forties with her grey hair piled neatly in a bun under her lace kerchief had replied "Your father wouldn't be too pleased, he wants you brought to be a great lady".

Susan knew she had won the argument then as Mrs O'Reilly only brought her father into it when she was beaten. So she smiled angelically at the old lady and said "Just a few minutes more and then I'll be happy". She thought of dear Papa and hoped there wasn't a storm in the Mediterranean tonight with his ship tossing and turning in the waves. Not that that would frighten Papa but all the same it would be safer if he was in port or on dry land somewhere, She hoped everyone was safe especially the new Queen. She had seen a picture of her in her coronation robes in the Illustrated London News. The nuns had shown it around the school.

She was so beautiful and regal, the most beautiful queen on earth. She was sure to visit Ireland and maybe Papa would have her presented to her in Dublin Castle, she would wear a fabulous ball gown herself and Papa would wear his naval uniform. They would dance with all the gentry and nobility in the castle. She was sure Papa would do it for her but she wouldn't mention it to Mrs O'Brien.

She prayed every night for the Queen and for her conversion to the true faith. Oh wouldn't that be one in the eye for all the Protestant gentry in Kildare and in Ireland! Maybe God would do it and surely all the people in England would follow her example and maybe Mr Daniel O'Connell would become the Lord Lieutenant, though she knew that was against the law but if Mr O'Connell demanded it, then it would happen and Ireland would be owned by the Catholics again. Papa would like that.

As the wind howled more fiercely she could hear the sash windows rattling in the whole house and banging against their frames. It seemed as if the entire building was shuddering. It was so exciting! What would the countryside look like tomorrow? How the poor horses must be frightened, but the grooms and stable boys would be with them calming then down. The storm must be all over Ireland now knocking old trees and blowing around everything that wasn't tied down in its wake. And the poor people, it would be a dreadful night for them. In spite of what Mrs O'Reilly had said, how awful it would be for them to have their frail little houses torn down. She would include them in her prayers tonight. She had heard the maids in the kitchen whisper that Mrs Brennan was going to have a baby. She pretended that she did not understand as she knew she wasn't supposed to know about babies and how they were made. But she knew alright, one of the big girls at school had told her amid screams and giggles of the other listeners. She had pretended to be disgusted but was fascinated by the great secret.

She didn't let on to anyone around here that she knew all about it, least of all Mrs O'Reilly. She knew it was unladylike to know such things not to mention discussing them and anyway she got more information if the servants believed she did not understand what they were talking about. Maybe the baby would be born tonight. What a strange night to come into the world! She added on Mrs Brennan's name to her list to pray for at bedtime and the poor little baby that might be born this very night. She'd have babies herself when she got married. Papa would find a match for her among the Catholic gentry in Kildare or maybe in Carlow. She hoped he wouldn't pick a man that would be too old and that he would be handsome and dashing and religious.

Someone just like her Papa but only younger, of course. Papa would see that it was all done properly. It would be lovely to be married! She would be lady of the house and look after her poor Mama who suffered from her nerves since the loss of her three children. Maybe her Papa would be retired from the Navy then and she would look after him too. She would have lots of children and call the first boy after her dead brother Dominick and of course, her father. She would go to balls and suppers with her husband and to the State occasions in Dublin Castle. They would go hunting together and look grand on their beautiful mounts with all the tenants coming out to watch and cheer them.

When Papa died she would own the house and lands at Kildangan but it was evil to think of that. Poor Papa, she hoped he would live to be a hundred and always be there to guide her. She shivered a little now, why did she have to have the evil, wicked thought of her dear Papa dying? All the houses and lands in Ireland would be worth nothing to her if anything happened to him. She would even become a nun if that's what he wanted but she hoped he didn't really. She felt a bit upset now and retired from the window closing the heavy drapes behind her.

Mrs O'Brien sat on a chair at the bedside waiting for her. Without speaking Susan knelt at the side of her bed and started her long list of prayers for the poor people this night, for the Queen and for her conversion to the true faith, for her Mama and Papa, for her dead brother and sisters and for her friends at school. Finally she rounded it all off with a "Hail, Holy Queen" for anyone she might have left out and then a prayer to her guardian angel for her own protection. "Angel of God, my guardian dear, to whom God's love commits me here, ever this day be at my side to love and guard, to rule and guide, Amen". "I'm ready for bed now Mrs O'Brien" she called to her nurse who was standing waiting for her at the bedside sliding the bedpan up and down under the covers to warm the bed for her young mistress.

She helped Susan out of her dressing gown and draped it over the bedside chair where it was within easy reach. Then Susan slipped quietly between the covers. "Goodnight sweet child and sleep tight" said the smiling nurse as she tucked her charge snugly in to the big bed. As she did the clock on the mantle chimed seven and Mrs. O'Brien, flickering candle in one hand and the cooling bedpan in the other, slipped quietly out of the bedroom. When she was sure she had left, Susan started to sob quietly in her bed, thinking of how wicked she had been to imagine her Papa dying and leaving her the estate. There had been enough deaths in her family and anyway she would rather die herself rather than have anything happen to Papa. She would say a whole Rosary for Papa's well-being and safety and to atone for her own selfishness and confess it on the First Friday. Outside the raging wind rose and fell continuously and the rattling of the windows making a noisy backdrop to Susan's attempt to nod off in her normally silent bedroom. Sobbing and praying and thinking of her father, Susan O'Reilly fell asleep.

Part III

Back in Willy Brennan's cabin the man of the house and the midwife were sitting beside the fire. In her arms was a naked baby boy. On the ground beside her was an uncorked bottle of Holy Water. "I baptise thee in the name of the father, son and Holy Ghost " crooned the midwife dotingly as she rubbed the Holy Water into his brow making a sign of the cross as she did so. "He's a grand little man," said his father adoringly while the child's bothered grandmother stared incomprehensibly at the bundle. "Is the milk warm yet?" the Widow Delaney asked "not boiling now mind". "It is for sure " answered Willy. "Then pour it into the jug and put in a small drop of the cratur and give it to Catherine, God knows she has earned it this night." Willy did as instructed and held the jug up to his exhausted wife's lips and she swallowed the warm milk and whiskey thirstily.

"He's a beauty alright "said Mrs. Delaney as she laid the baby in his mother's arms "Took after his Mammy" she added mischievously. "I told you your Mammy would in heaven would see you through". Catherine could only manage a faint smile as she snuggled the baby to her breast and prepared to give him his first suckle. Meanwhile Mrs Delaney and Willy were back at the fire. "Aren't you going to ask me if I have a mouth on me?" asked the delighted midwife. "I'm sorry, Mrs Delaney, you'll have a drop of whiskey?" Willy asked. The thatch was rising now and the room was half filled with smoke. The old woman was now snoozing, making a rattling wheezing sound. "Surely you have a pipe on a night like tonight?" "Surely" said Willy as he meekly got a clay pipe from the dresser. "Give us a pull," said Catherine sitting up in her bed.

Willy went over to his wife and gave her the first smoke after he had put a tiny coal into the white pipe. It had "Erin go Bragh" outlined in relief on it. He then passed it to Mrs Delaney. There was hardly any tobacco left in it when it was his turn but he didn't care. The women were happy and so was he. Outside the tempest raged but inside the Brennan's cabin all was peace and serenity as Willy and the Widow Delaney settled down to a few scoops and a pipe to celebrate the night's proceedings.

While his wife and baby slept, Willy outlined his plans for his son to Mrs Delaney. He was going to call his first-born Tom and that he would go to school and learn to read, write and reckon as well as the best of them. "And what good would all that book learning be to him? Sure it's a fighter you want him to be, like the great Dan Donnelly, the greatest Kildare man that ever lived. I saw him box in the Curragh in 1815. He bate the living daylights out of the Englishman George Cooper. It was a great day for Ireland. I remember it well though I was only a slip of a girl. Now there was a real man and rich too from his prize-fights, the purse that day was twenty guineas." "Go away out of that Mrs Delaney. I've heard all those yarns about Dan Donnelly a hundred times before. There was never a fighter in this family, it's a scholar he'll be, he'll make something out of his life and not be a slave to the landowners like me and his forefathers "

"What are you talking about you foolish gossoon, sure you are not a slave and neither was your father before you, sure don't you work for the O'Reillys and aren't you and yours respected all over Kildangan and beyond?" replied the old crone, genuinely perplexed. "Aye" answered Willy "and we could be kicked out on the road at the whim of Miss O'Reilly with only the ditch to sleep in, not that she would of course, she is a decent lady and wouldn't do that, but she could if she wanted to, that's no way to live." "It's the way it is and always was, what other way could it be, do you want the fairies to gift you with a crock of gold?" The sulky head of Willy Brennan didn't reply, no point in trying to reason with this good, stupid woman but her words meant nothing to him. He meant what he said, his son would have a better life that he or his fathers before him had, slaving away for a landowner until he dropped. The wizened midwife was now in talkative form as the whiskey loosened her tongue, not that it needed much loosening.

She set herself to explain to Willy the reason for the dreadful storm that was now demolishing the countryside. "It was the fairies that done it" she said authoritatively, "Haven't they every right to be displeased with all those new railways being built through their lands and tracks" Willy sat silently listening, he had heard it all before. "The English and the bigshots in Dublin know nothing about the fairies and couldn't care less but they will after tonight when all their shiny railways and smoky engines are blown away as far as kingdom come." Willy nodded in agreement. He too, was afraid of the fairies and their dreadful curses though he was ashamed to admit it but he loved the railways too. Weren't they new and wonderful, so enormous and so fast? Soon those coaches and Bianconi cars that carried people all over the country would be a thing of the past not to talk of the poor people who couldn't afford a coach fare walking from place to place, that would all end in time and no harm either. People would travel from town to town on a train, hard to imagine but a lovely prospect and so exciting and so fast.

He hoped one day to travel on one, maybe as far as Dublin just for the thrill of it though he couldn't imagine that he would ever have business to do in the city but he would love to do it all the same. But he didn't want to annoy Mrs Delaney; she had been so good this night, it was a great reassurance to know that his wife was in such safe hands at such a dangerous time as childbirth. So for peace sake he kept quiet. That was his way, a quiet mouth saved so much trouble and annoyance, it worked well for him all his life so far.

The two of them rambled on into the small hours of the morning, while the storm raged on the outside, sometimes shaking the roof but it held firm. This filled Willy with satisfaction as he knew this would not be the case with so many other roofs in Kildangan. He took a

more than slight satisfaction from the idea that his neighbours would suffer for not being as diligent in their preparations for the storm as he was. Inside was filled with smoke from the strong downdraught but nobody minded.
In fact, the tempest outside made them feel safe, secure and warm inside. Making less and less sense as the jug of whiskey was drained, Willy now had the warm feeling of intoxication as he listened smiling to the midwife's rambling. Meanwhile Catherine slept quietly with her newborn baby, quiet as a lamb and his mother snored softly in the corner.

It seemed as if the storm had abated somewhat by the time they went to bed or at least so it appeared to them in their now merry condition. The baby slept quietly in his mother's arms.
The Widow Delaney lifted him remarkably gently and expertly for a drunken hag from the breast of her mother. She placed him snugly in the crib that had been left beside the bed. It was the same crib that Willy had slept in when he was an infant made from an orange box by his father many years previously.

Mrs Delaney awkwardly climbed over the sleeping mother and got into bed on the far side, removing only her shawl and pinafore and putting then on top of her. Willy gently eased himself in on the near side, slipping off his jacket and boots and opening the waistband of his breeches. He had placed his old mother in the only chair in the room, away from the fire to make sure she didn't fall in. She would sleep soundly there until the morning. He had no fear of her in that regard.

After what seemed like hours later, Willy was wakened by his wife's stirring. He beamed at her in the almost darkened cabin, no doubt she had been disturbed by Mrs Delaney's snoring which was now as loud as the storm outside. Catherine looked so beautiful now in the soft light of the dying fire, dreamingly he felt a stirring in his crotch for her.
He got up on one elbow and looked into her green, sleep filled and exhausted eyes while he whispered to her "I think you're a grand girl altogether." The answer was swift and strong. "Don't even dream about it Willy Brennan, I'm all sore down there, touch me and I'll bate the head off you." From the other side of the bed came "Leave her alone you dirty rascal, don't touch her for a week or you'll have no luck" Mrs Delaney had joined in.

"Mind your own business, you old hag and go back to sleep" answered Willly as he moved onto his back. He smiled as he turned over and went asleep, he just loved a woman with the spirit of his Catherine. There would be plenty of time for riding when she got her strength back.

Chapter 2

A Famine Wedding.

Leinster Express 21st November 1849:
*... **The wedding of Charles Edward More O'Ferrall Esq., fifth son of Major Ambrose More O'Ferrall of Balyna Castle, County Kildare and Mistress Susan O'Reilly of Kildangan House, daughter of Commander Dominick O'Reilly (deceased) late of Her Majesty's Navy, will take place in the Roman Catholic Chapel in Kildangan, Co. Kildare on Thursday 29th November 1849 at 8.00am.***

"Its so exciting." Catherine Brennan was talking to herself and in a state of nervous anticipation as she moved smartly around her neat kitchen, getting the dinner ready for the men. They would be in soon, it was near the middle of the day and she would soon hear the estate bell dismissing them for their grub. She had a big pot of India Meal flavoured with a few carrots, turnips and salt on the crane over the open fire. "I wonder if they have any news," she said out loud. The wedding was tomorrow and she was sure that it would be the most wonderful thing she would ever see in her life.

The Lady was going to wear a dress of pure silk made for her in Dublin and the material had come all the way from Hindustan, imagine the heathens in those faraway places making material for a wedding dress in Kildangan! Miss O'Reilly would look like a princess which she kind of was really but the men didn't care about that, or so they said. But she knew that her Willy was just as excited about the wedding as she was but he wouldn't admit it. It wasn't manly to care about such things, it just wasn't. They would have a great day tomorrow; it wasn't like they were getting married themselves, gentry weddings were different, but you could imagine, there was no harm in that, being a beautiful, rich young lady and having a grand wedding .

She didn't like it that the dress was going to be white. That was the colour that all the gentry wore at their weddings nowadays just because Queen Victoria of England had worn one at her wedding to the German Prince Albert. It was bad luck wearing a white dress at a wedding as Victoria would learn to her cost, Catherine was sure of that. These things were true for kings and queens as they were for the common people. November though, was a good month to get married in, so they said. She would be happy.

But the marriage day was all wrong. She remembered the rhyme which told you when to marry: "Monday for health, Tuesday for wealth, Wednesday the best day of all, Thursday for losses, Friday for crosses, Saturday for no luck at all" Thursday: a wedding day for losses, she hoped poor Miss O'Reilly would not suffer for her choice of that day. How stupid people were to ignore these old pisheogues! They came down to us from the wisdom of the old people and it was foolish to ignore them. Surely it wouldn't have caused any inconvenience to marry on a Wednesday? But Miss O'Reilly was a very religious lady and didn't care for the old customs. Catherine hoped to God that things wouldn't go against her and bring her bad luck, she was a kind and efficient landowner and her workers and tenants never went hungry even in these hard times with the potato crop failing and the poor people dying of hunger and disease all over the country. Herself and Willy and the children prayed for Miss O'Reilly every night.

The Lady was not like the More O'Ferrrals, into whom she was marrying even though they were gentry too. People said that in spite of their airs and graces, they didn't have a pot to piss in, and if they had they would miss it anyway. No wonder they were so cock-a-hoop about their match with the Lady. The gentry were always trying to marry above their station not like the common people who were happy to marry one another even though they owned nothing except maybe a few sticks of furniture and their children. Yes indeed, Susan O'Reilly was a great catch for the More O'Ferralls.

Miss O'Reilly had land and money and they had nothing except their name and history. Willy said that they came from a great family descended from the High Kings of Ireland but a lot of good that was, Catherine thought. That didn't mean they knew how to run a great place like Kildangan, a lot of these gentry lived above their means and that meant misery for their tenants and farmworkers. Some of them got into so much debt that they ruined their estates and destroyed their fortunes.

The O'Reillys knew how to run the demesne and nobody could take that from them. The Mistress had run the whole place on her own since her father had died in '45 and his father and grandfather had run the place since God knows when. What woman in Ireland could do a thing like that, Catherine wondered? There were lots of men who couldn't do it either in spite of all their ould strutting around like cocks of the walk.
Still she had to find a husband though. A woman in her position couldn't remain single and become an old maid. It wasn't that she was short of offers, not with a fortune like hers. There was no fear of her ending up on the shelf. All the same it was a pity she had to marry such an old man. Mr More O'Ferrall was forty-four, they said. Catherine wondered if she would get any babies from an ould lad like that.

Of course they all said "the older the fiddle the sweeter the tune " but she wondered what an old man like that would be able for in the marriage bed. Then again, there weren't many Catholic gentry around and even a great lady like Miss O'Reilly wouldn't have much choice and she couldn't marry a Protestant without endangering her faith and her soul. A religious lady like her wouldn't do a thing like that.
Maybe in marriage it was better to be a common person like herself. She had picked Willy out from all the boys and never regretted her choice. She had known him all her life and watched him grow into a fine, strapping lad. She remembered staring at him at Mass that Sunday

morning long ago even though she had seen him many times before around Kildangan, but there was something about him that morning. And then he stared back. Immediately she knew that it was not just her fancy, he wanted her too.

All of a sudden she felt that he was the one for her, she still remembered the tingling feeling she got when she realised that and was afraid that someone in the chapel would notice. She felt her cheeks redden and her body twitched all over and she could feel her heartbeat quicken. God! She had that feeling again now, as she walked around her kitchen. Willy Brennan was still a fine man after all these years. She remembered well asking her mother what she would do.

Her mother gave her a deep searching look but replied without hesitation "Take him walking and let nature take its course" and then almost as an afterthought said "Are you completely sure?" when Catherine replied that yes she was never so sure of anything, her mother said "Then take him down to the Courtin' Tree on the riverbank this very night and if he's a man at all he'll make all the moves after that. That's where your father and I did it for the very first time" Catherine felt her face flush and her heart beat faster. So much information in one go but she had no hesitation in making up her mind. Tonight would be the night. First she must give herself a good scrubbing in rainwater, which was the best for a clear complexion, and especially good down there. She ran out the door, grabbing a basin along the way. Just outside the house she spotted a man coming up the lane. It was Willy, he looked at her sheepishly and asked "Catherine, do you want to come walking with me tonight?" He wasn't the first she had done it with at the Courtin' Tree but she knew in her heart that this was really going to be different.

She was confident that he felt that way too or else he would not have come up to the house in broad daylight all scrubbed up and still in his Sunday Best.
He arrived after the tea and walked straight into the kitchen. He looked so smart she thought, as she conjured up his outfit that evening in her mind's eye. He wore knee britches of black and a scarlet jacket. He looked quite a macaroni, she thought, smiling to herself. Thank God she had on her red dress as her mother told her with the tight laced-up bodice. "That will get him going alright" Mammy had said. Her father was somewhat surprised to see Willy Brennan, all dressed up in his kitchen and visiting his daughter but copped on soon enough when he saw that her mother was in on the business.

"They are a decent family, the Brennans, he won't let her down" he had said to his wife when they had left. It had been magic that first time with Willy Brennan on the riverbank in Kildangan under the Courtin' Tree on that warm summer's night. He had taken her manfully and she gave herself willingly once the initial shyness and fumbling in the removal of their clothes and their shyness in seeing each other's private parts. She gave herself with an abandon she had never shown before.

With the other boys she had always held something back but with Willy she had let go completely even to the point of moaning with pleasure when he hit the spot. God! she had moaned like a cow being serviced by the bull in Miss O'Reilly's orchard. She hadn't allowed herself to do that with the other boys, she hadn't felt like it anyway. They would have thought they were doing her a favour instead of the other way around. Anyway they would tell all their friends. They were a right crowd of gossipmongers and boasters, the boys in Kildangan.

They had both been silent on the way home, but this had been a silence of mutual understanding. When they got to her door, he asked "Will you come out with me again tomorrow night, Catherine?" and she replied without hesitation "I will Willy Brennan and every night after that if you want" She stood by the door and watched him run down the lane, skipping and jumping like a child. She went inside with a smile on her face to give a full report to her mother. Now as she stood in her kitchen in Kildangan, a full eleven years later she felt the same thrill as she felt as she walked down that riverbank with her man.

Her two youngest children Katie and Nicholas raced into the kitchen and chanted rhythmically "Daddy and Tommy are coming up the road, the ro-ad, the ro-ad." "Clear out now the pair of you or I'll give a belt" said Catherine. She was vexed now, she had missed the estate bell with her daydreaming and the men were about to come in and she didn't have the table set. She hated being caught out like that. She got the bowls from the dresser and banged them down on the table and grabbed the pot from the crane over the fire. Just as she was spooning out the India meal stew her husband Willy and her eldest son Tommy walked in the door and without a word plonked themselves at the table. When she had finished spooning out the stew, she got two spoons from the dresser and handed them to her men. Then she scooped out a mug of buttermilk from the pail and put it between the two.

"Well, come on you two, have you any news?" "Divil a bit" said Willy hardly able to suppress a smile. He really knew how to annoy a woman, thought Catherine. Sometimes she felt like strangling him and she waiting all morning to find out what was happening. Himself and Tommy started to eat their dinner in silence while Catherine hovered over them in obvious annoyance at her husband's silence. Only the slurping sound of their eating filled the small cabin. At last when he knew his wife would take no more, Willy spoke. "There must be hundreds of people up at the Big House," he said. "So you've got a tongue in your head then have you? I thought the cat got it for awhile" replied Catherine. "No need for that at all now, wife," smiled Willy. "They're carrying in all sorts of fancy things in, food and wines and fancy cloths. Some of the carts have come all the way from Dublin. They travelled through the night and the barn is being got ready for the workmen and tenants, everything is being cleared out, for the dancing and eating, there will be all sorts of food, enough to feed an army and drink too. The O'Reillys have never been short when it comes to hospitality, and dancing. Three fiddlers have been hired, three, it'll be the best day in Kildangan for years." "I hope to God the weather holds fine for them" said Catherine. "Indeed it will," said Willy. "Will there be spuds and all?" asked Tommy. "No, I don't think so, even though the crop wasn't all ruined this year" replied Willy. "Anyway, potatoes are finished in this country for all time, there's no cure for the blight, there will be no spuds in Ireland from now on unless they're taken in from out foreign. The day of the potato is finished in this country and no harm either, that's all the poor people used to eat, morning noon and night, God help them. But don't worry son, there will be plenty of bread and apples and meats".

"But what will the poor people eat now that they have no potatoes?" asked Tommy, getting into his stride. "I suppose they will have to make do with what the rest of us eat, bread and honey" replied his father, smiling teasingly at his son. "We don't eat bread and honey" said Tommy, looking mystified at his father. "The King was in the Counting House, counting out his money, The Queen was in the parlour eating bread and honey, The maid was in the yard putting out clothes When along came a blackbird and pecked off her nose " recited Willy as his son looked on in exasperation at him. Daddies can be very annoying, thought Tommy.

"Anyway, we'll have a great day tomorrow up at the house, a day to remember, all the style of the county and beyond will be there. All the workmen are having a day off after we look after the stock and Mr Fitzgerald said that the outdoor men would be allowed into the chapel with their wives". "Oh my God" said Catherine "into the chapel, are you pulling my leg Willy Brennan, because if you are I'll never talk to you again, as sure as God's my judge?"

"Its true alright, they couldn't know before but seemingly Miss O'Reilly has insisted. She said that the Chapel had been built by her grandfather for the workers on his estate as well as his own family and that she wasn't going to keep them out on the most important day of her life. God bless the little woman. I hope you've something nice to wear." "I'd never let you down, Willy Brennan" said Catherine, now close to tears at the excitement of it all and furious at her husband's last remark.

Willy, who knew her change of moods only too well now, and thought that maybe his teasing had gone too far, sought to reassure her. "I'm sure you'll be grand." "Grand?" said Catherine with the tears now rolling down her cheeks in anger, frustration and excitement, "I've only being saving my new bonnet for over a year for this and new britches for you, what kind of a woman do you think I am Willy Brennan?"
Willy was now totally defeated in the face of his wife's tears and dropped his head into his food. Catherine, now sensing victory, wiped away her tears with her cuff and managed a smile. "I'll be the best looking woman in Kildangan, I'll turn their heads, just wait till you see me in my new bonnet, You'll be proud as punch of me, Willy Brennan" "Oh my God deliver me from women" said Willy as he looked across the table for support

from his son who smiled sympathetically back at him but was delighted with his mother. He was still annoyed at being caught out with the nursery rhyme. They were for children and he was now working in the yard and wanted to be treated as a grown-up.

Tommy was a strapping light brown haired young man of nearly eleven years. He had been working with his father in the yard of the big house since he turned ten. He took his new station in life very seriously. "Will the new Master be good to us all, the way the O'Reillys were?" asked Tommy, who, well used to his parents' love tussles, knew that the only way out was to change the subject. "Indeed he will with the help of God" replied Willy. "Sure won't Miss O'Reilly be at his side to make sure nothing changes. Haven't we been living to the best with never a day hungry when the poor people in the west and south of Ireland are starving to death and eating the grass itself, the poor creatures?"

"Why are they eating grass, Daddy, why don't they eat carrots or turnips?" asked his son, still trying to figure out the mystery of why the poor people were starving. "All they ever had was potatoes and now the crops are rotten with the blight disease, they are so poor they have nothing else, all they ever lived on was spuds with a bit of salt or butter if they had it. There are thousands of them, they have loads of children and no land or employment. It was bound to happen sooner or later" he told his son in a quiet and guilty voice. He was very proud of his son though he was disappointed that he wasn't more of a scholar and had left school so early, he had hoped that he would stick with his books and build a better life for himself than working on the land like himself and his fathers before him.

"Its nothing to boast about that we can't feed our own people even if they are poor and backward" interjected his mother, "It's a terrible thing that's happening in the country but it's the will of God, I suppose and that's the end of it, there's nothing can be done about it"
"If it's the will of God then He has a very strange way of going on, all those poor people dying of hunger and disease, isn't he supposed to love the poor especially? The potato was the curse of this country letting all those people live on hardly any land at all but I suppose at the end of the day there will be more food and land for the rest of us. Maybe that's the will of God but its terrible to think of the suffering of all the poor families that are being wiped out" her husband interjected. He paused and looked at his son as if imagining what would happen to him if he could not put food on the table.

"But I suppose you're right; the will of God, but it's a terrible thing the will of God" continued her husband "I hate talking about it, it makes me feel guilty as if we all had something to do with it. We are never going to talk about this again" Now he looked down at his plate of India meal stew as if he was still thinking about his own and his wife's words. Tommy couldn't take in all in what was said about the poor people dying of hunger while he and his Mammy and Daddy were sitting here eating their dinner, if he knew a poor boy he would give him half his dinner, all he knew for sure was that he was never to bring up the issue again.

He knew that his father was upset by this talk and that he meant what he said about not talking about it again. "They say in the yard that the More O'Ferralls are great gentry altogether and that they care more about their horses than they do about their tenants". Tommy said, yet again trying to change the subject. "Don't be listening to talk like that, Tommy my son, the More O'Ferralls are a great Irish family going back to times before the English came, they'll look after us alright."
"Do the More O'Ferralls talk in Irish?" asked Tommy, much taken by the new landlord's ancestry.
"Not at all, my boy" answered his father indulgently, "Where did you get that idea into your head? Only the poor people of the West speak in Irish. The More O'Ferralls are great gentry, all the great gentry talk in English like us, even the great Daniel O'Connell, the Liberator".

"Its bad luck all the same for them to be marrying on a Thursday and in November too" said Catherine now back in the flow of conversation. "Miss O'Reilly doesn't believe in those pisheogues," said Willy. "The Liberator, may the Lord have mercy on his soul, wanted us to get rid of all those old superstitions and the O'Reillys like all the Irish gentry and the rest of us followed him." "Why did he want us to do that?" asked Tommy. "He wanted Ireland to be a modern country and to put behind us all the old backward ways, he was a great man" his father answered. "Still there's no point in leaving all those old customs, there must be

something in them, there's no point in tempting fate, a wedding
before Lent and a gorgeous, red silk dress wouldn't have killed them" countered Catherine.

Part II

It was still dark, though the drapes had been opened as Mrs O'Brien brushed her young mistress' chestnut brown hair by candlelight in front of the angled mirror on the dressing table. Stouter now and delighting in her girth, after thirty years of service she had been promoted to Lady's Maid, a position of which she was immensely proud and she used it to look down her nose at all the other indoor staff, whom she considered occupied positions far inferior to hers. "Hush Alanna, what has you so sad on this the morning of the best day of your life?"

Susan O'Reilly continued to stare grimly into the mirror. She had been up since four and had already bathed right here in her bedroom in front of the fire and was washed down from head to toe by Mrs O'Brien as she stood shivering in the zinc tub, now she felt cold and apprehensive. "I don't know Mrs O'Brien, it must be the worry of it all, I feel so lonely." "Well you won't be lonely for long, today you'll be the fairest bride in the country, the envy of all and the wife of a great gentleman."

"You don't think he's too old for me? I know that's what they're saying behind my back." "Indeed and they're not and if there are some that are, sure it's only jealousy, any lady would give her right hand to be wedded to Mr More O'Ferrall and as for his age then the older the fiddle the sweeter the tune, that's what I say and it's true. As you'll find out for yourself tonight." She added knowingly and smiling sweetly at her charge.

Susan managed a weak smile in response. "I'm a bit nervous about that part too," she said watching for Mrs O'Brien's reaction in the mirror. "Don't fret yourself about that my chicken, it will all come natural to you." "What if I don't know what to do?" asked Susan getting to the heart of the matter. "You don't have to do anything at all my lovely, is that what's worrying you? Sure you just have to lie there. It's up to the man to do all the work in that department. It's the only time they have to do any work" she chuckled. "But won't it hurt awfully?" asked Susan now wide eyed with interest. "Who told you that? I hope you haven't been listening to those trollops in the kitchen, its hurts a bit at first, but after that its all plain sailing. That's the way it was with my poor departed Jim, may the Lord have mercy on his soul. You might even get to like it after awhile. It's nature's way." "I don't think I ever could like it Mrs O'Brien, it's too disgusting, the idea of a man poking around down there" "You'll change your mind my Lady, mark my words, it's only the same as getting your hair brushed, a bit sore at first but then nice and pleasant" and they both giggled. "Thanks Mrs O'Brien" said Susan, now feeling a little better, just like getting her hair brushed, well now that couldn't be too bad!

Mrs O'Brien continued her long downward stokes bringing a sheen to Susan's brown hair. "You have a cup of tea now and put plenty of sugar in it, that won't break your fast at all. It will be a good few hours before the Wedding Breakfast and we don't want you going weak in the Chapel. It's happened before to many a young woman. I'll be in with the dressers in awhile, it will take an hour or so to get you into your gown and you'll look like the Queen of Sheba. It'll be bright soon and we won't feel the morning passing".

She bent down and kissed her Lady on the cheek, something she hadn't done since she was a child. Susan felt all warm and reassured at the gentle touch and soapy smell of her maid. As Mrs O'Brien left the room it was her turn to sob gently for the loss of innocence of her dear mistress. As she was leaving Susan called to her "Mrs O'Brien, please send up Sparks."

Susan smiled at herself in the mirror and picked up the silver-backed hairbrush. She was a funny woman Mrs O'Brien even though she didn't mean to be. It was just like getting your hair brushed! She stroked its handle. "I hope to God his brush isn't too big" she said out loud and then started to laugh until the tears ran came into her eyes. She stopped abruptly as she heard a sharp knock on the door.

"Come in Sparks" she called. The English butler entered the room and bowed stiffly as he approached her. She had employed him just a year ago for this very day. He would know how to do things with style, not like her poor, loyal Irish servants. Adopting her stern face she asked, "Sparks is everything in order for this morning?" "Yes Ma'am" he replied, "The servants have been up all night. The beeves and hams are still cooking, the fowl are cooling, perfectly finished, the kitchen is working to order, all the staff present and correct. The Wedding Cakes are laid out and the wines are decanted. All is set for your happy return from the Chapel at 9.00." "I don't think the Wedding Party will be back by then Sparks, but better be ready anyway, is everything outside prepared?" "Fitzgerald is in charge of outdoor arrangements Ma'am," he replied haughtily making it clear that he resented having anything to do with the home farm workers whom he considered to be of inferior status to his own and to the house staff.

"Please communicate with him and make sure that everything is in order" she commanded.
"And Sparks make sure that none of the coachmen break their fast, I won't have my wedding day marred by sacrilege." "Even those who do not intend to receive the Communion, my Lady?" "Yes, you must make sure of this, it is most important. The coaches will be arriving soon. The same goes for the gentlefolk too, make sure there are no beverages on view in the Drawing Room, there is to be no imbibing until the wedding ceremony is over" "Even for members of the Established Church Ma'am?" asked Sparks cheekily. "Yes Sparks, including our Protestant friends and neighbours" rejoined Susan, flushing slightly "This is a Catholic household, make sure that these rules are followed exactly" If Sparks felt humiliated by this put down, he didn't show it and remained stony faced. "Mr More O'Ferrall will arrive presently, show him to the main bedroom where he may wish to relax in privacy for awhile until it is time to head for the Chapel, tell me immediately he arrives." "Indeed, Ma'am, will that be all?"

"Thank you Sparks, that will be all." As he withdrew Susan emitted a sigh of relief; relations with her butler were more like a duel between equals than a conversation between mistress and servant, but though he was cold and formal, he was efficient and competent and he knew how to organise an affair like this. She wasn't sorry she was sharp with him, he could be impertinent in his own stiff way, the English were like that. As Sparks passed out through the door, the dressers and the seamstress, led by Mrs O'Brien walked past him without knocking.

"Are you ready, my Lady?" asked her maid. "Ready as I'll ever be" replied Susan getting to her feet. Then the ceremony and ordeal of getting into her gown began. The stiff linen petticoats went over her head making a wide circle of fabric about her feet and tapering up to her waist. The tight whalebone bodice around her waist accentuated her slim figure, her wasp waist and small bosom. Last of all she was fitted with her luxurious white silk gown, embroidered with shamrocks. Their bright green colour made them stand out remarkably against the whiteness of the silk. Its sleeves were tight at the wrists and full and flouncy on the sleeves. It went up to her neck modestly but embarrassingly exaggerated her bosom and was matched by a generous bustle at the rear. A V-shape was made out in cream piping on front and back, interspersed with cream buttons and at the back was a hanging v-shaped flap. Looking down she could see what seemed like yards and yards of embroidered silk stretching down to the ground. This was the best part, now she did really feel like a bride. The women gasped and smiled in admiration and the seamstress started to make some last minute alterations and to sew Susan O'Reilly into her wedding dress.

A knock on the door was answered by Mrs O'Brien who returned with the news that Mr More O'Ferrall had arrived and was waiting downstairs in the main drawing room.
His propriety seemingly did not allow him to take possession of the main bedroom until after the ceremony, the news of which made Susan smile with pride and more than a small bit of embarrassment at the moral correctness of her husband-to-be. But he was right of course, all cause for gossip must be avoided.
"Tell him that I shall be down presently," she said, realising again that soon she would no longer be in command of Kildanagan House. In a few hours time she would be Mrs Charles Edward More O'Ferrall and the happiest woman in Ireland.
Her gown now fitted, she had been standing for almost an hour and a half and as the women started to work on her hair, Susan's mood changed. Her hair was now parted in the middle, smoothed down and made into ringlets at the sides with the heated curling tongs. As her hair singed, she thought of the More O'Ferralls and how scathing her beloved father had been of them.

They had been lukewarm in their support for Daniel O'Connell, aping the Catholic aristocrats who were contemptuous of Mr. O'Connell's middle class status, to them a barrister was really not far removed from being an ordinary tradesman. His popularity and support among the common people and the lower classes too, was despised by them and considered to be little short of vulgar and democratic. It was just jealousy of his achievements, they had done so little in the past 50 years with their loyal petitions to the King asking for Catholic rights which always fell on the deaf ears of the bigoted and more than half mad old King George. When that pompous little local bishop of Kildare and Leighlin, James Doyle or JKL as he liked to be called, had attacked O'Connell over Catholic education, they had rowed right in behind him. Sitting in his palace called "Braganza" in Carlow, typical of his breed living in the past, calling his palace after the Portuguese Royal family, they could not see that the world had changed. A lot the Portuguese Royal Family mattered to the people of Ireland who were trying to better themselves under O'Connell.

After all he had done for the Catholics of Ireland; winning Emancipation for them almost single-handed while their own upper classes were sitting on their backsides for the last hundred years sending loyal petitions to the King and secretly hoping that the Stuarts would return to the throne and establish a new regime that would see them replace the Protestant ascendancy.

It had made her father so angry. The bishop's successor, Dr Healy was not asked to officiate at her wedding; it would dishonour her father's memory. There were some things on which she would not bend. The More O'Ferralls had even called her husband-to-be after the

Stuart Pretender. The Stuarts had been driven from England, Scotland and Ireland not only because of their Catholic Faith but also because they couldn't accept the reality that the English and Scottish were almost all Protestants now. Talk about living in the past! Yes, she would change that, her household would be modern and support O'Connell's successor whoever that might be. And that idiot of a Richard More O'Ferrall who was appointed the Governor of Malta, through O'Connell's intercession. He was the first Catholic Governor to be appointed in the Empire for 150 years. What did he go and do? After a row with the natives who wanted a union with Italy, he went and resigned. Resigned!. Her face reddened with anger, such ingratitude and stupidity, resigned! That's why she postponed the wedding till November. She would put some backbone into that family, her sons would not be resigners, they would be fighters like dear Papa! She had run the estate since Papa's death and not a family had been evicted or gone hungry, even during the last few difficult years when the potato crop had failed. Other landlords were facing bankruptcy and their tenants starvation and through their own fault entirely.

She had kept her estate in credit during the last few difficult years and her rents, in Kildare at least, had held up. Her tenants had done well, returning a tidy profit on their cattle and corn sales. What other woman in Ireland had done the same? None. Well maybe Miss Maria Edgeworth in Longford had but she had money from the books she had written, that would have made it easier for her.

She would show them. The wedding today would show all of Kildare and beyond what stuff the O'Reillys were made of. Even if their name would die out with her marriage to the More O'Ferralls their spirit would continue through her children. She must have looked distracted or unwell as the servants around her began to cast concerned glances at her. "Are you alright, my Lady? You don't feel a bit faint?" asked a worried Mrs O'Brien.

"I feel ready to take on the whole world" replied a beaming Susan, now totally recovered from her distraction. "Go and see that the barouche is ready and make sure the cover is down so that we can be seen." "Are you sure, my Lady?" Mrs O'Brien knitted her brow with worry "It's perishing with the cold, my Lady."
"I'm sure, the tenants will want to see me on this of all days, and their new Master too" added Susan, almost as an afterthought, while at the same time admiring her beautiful coiffure in the mirror held in front of her. Yes, she looked gorgeous, her dear father would have been proud of her.

Everything was now ready, only the white lace shawl had now to be fitted. It was draped on her shoulders and the centre raised to cover her head where it was fastened by mother-of-pearl headed pins in her hair. "Tell Sparks, that I am now about to go down" she said to Mrs O'Brien who walked smartly out of the room with the news, looking so proud that it could have been her own wedding procession that she was about to announce. On her return Susan straightened her shoulders lifted the hem of her dress and then paused as she said a silent Hail Mary for the success of the day, then she walked out onto the landing. As she did her dressers murmured gently "Best wishes, my Lady" and Susan smiled nervously back at them. She stood at the top of her staircase in Kildangan House and looked down at her guests who were pouring out of the Drawing Room to witness her descent.

Standing first at the bottom of the staircase was her husband-to-be, Charles More O'Ferrall. She looked at him for a moment and with just a trace of a smile on his face which she deciphered as pride at what he was seeing. She took a deep breath, then graciously, one step at a time she descended the staircase as she did so the whole house seemed to erupt in a roar of cheers and hurrahs as she headed downstairs and into the main hall.

The Wedding Party left Kildangan House at 7.30am sharp with the carriages of the local gentry following behind the bride and groom's carriage. There was weak morning sunshine, in spite of it being late in the year, that was a good sign, she thought. The carriages made a grand procession as they drove down the freshly gravelled driveway and out onto Chapel Road. The coachman was perfectly turned out in grey greatcoat piped in green and top hat. The two grey mares that pulled the carriage trotted in perfect rhythm.

True to her wishes, the cover of the carriage was down and though shivering, she beamed at the estate workers on the avenue and the villagers on the road outside. They cheered her on with roars of approval and admiration. Her spouse to-be, Charles Edward More O'Ferrall sitting stiffly and silently beside her played his part and even forced a smile and waved as well, but she supposed he was nervous too. She was re-assured that he seemed more anxious than she was, it showed a vulnerable part of his nature. But she could see that his parents Major Ambrose and Mrs Alice More O'Ferrall, sitting stony-faced on the opposite seats were not impressed at the cheers of the common people which they knew were not for them. She was still the Lady of Kildanagan House. The louder the roar the more discomfited they seemed. Susan wished it would snow on them and waved back more enthusiastically than ever.

When they reached the Chapel, Susan and Charles were in right good form. He had loosened up considerably and though he had never said a word since they left Kildangan House he manfully took her by the arm and amid the thunderous applause and cheers led her into the small chapel. Chairs had been borrowed from the neighbouring big houses for the gentry and were placed in front of the altar rails.

Behind them the estate workers and tenants stood in a throng, disrespectfully talking and joking and swelling the small building to capacity. She could feel the spirits of her ancestors here in this small but perfectly proportioned chapel and especially she felt the presence of her beloved father. Her grandfather had built this place for his family and tenants; there had only been a thatched hall here before; not suitable for priest and congregation or the Holy Sacrifice of the Mass but all that the poor Catholics could afford during the previous century of religious oppression and penal laws. She had worshipped with her father here on countless occasions, what happy and sad memories that brought back!

The choir, which she had sent from her old school in Dublin sang hauntingly and beautifully and the lovely Latin intonations of the Parish Priest, Mr Michael Ryan made her swell with happiness and fulfilment. Here she was with the man who was to be her husband for ever. He was at her side and they were in the presence of God who resided in the tabernacle just feet away from where she sat. It was as if she had fallen into a perfect, magic trance.

The Wedding ceremony itself took place in the centre of the Chapel with the congregation welling around. Then it was back to the altar for Holy Communion and the rest of the Mass. How sweet the Host tasted on her tongue that morning! Charles, kneeling beside her looked almost stately in his black britches, cream silk waistcoat embroidered too with shamrocks, and his high collar and bow. But it was his emerald green velvet jacket that set his grey hair off. He was a handsome man indeed in spite of his age, she thought. Then she promised to love, honour and obey her husband and had the gold band placed on her finger as a symbol of their unity and fidelity. Suddenly it was all over and a feeling of panic and anti-climax hit her. Fortunately she knew exactly what to do and standing up she extended her left hand to her new husband who took it gracefully and led her through the parted congregation to the outside.

At the doors of the Chapel, the local gentlemen stood with their fowling pieces, barrels stuffed with downy feathers. When the bridal pair emerged they set off their guns and the loud and startling bang was followed by a shower of tiny feathers falling from the sky and a huge cheer from all around. Though Susan effected to be startled, she knew that this was a show of welcome and acceptance from the local gentry for her new husband and she had expected it. Everyone was smiling, everyone was happy, this is the way the world should always be, thought Susan, as happy as she was and surrounded by the well wishing inhabitants of her beloved Kildangan and of and the ladies and gentlemen of south Kildare. In the chilly morning air they re-mounted their carriage and, then set off back to the house for the Wedding Breakfast.

But first they drove through their village of Kildangan. It was important so show herself and her new husband to the peasantry. They expected that and Susan would not disappoint them, it was an important day for the people Kildangan as well as for herself.
The neat little cottages, freshly whitewashed on her instructions and some even newly thatched. The straw on the roofs was shining like gold in the weak winter's sun. The houses were fronted by the waving, cheering and smiling tenants and their children, all scrubbed up and looking respectable and wearing their best clothes. They shared her happiness and pride, what good people they were, so loyal, so loving!
Her breast heaved with pride at what she saw and she

believed that her new husband couldn't fail to be impressed. At a trot the horses moved on, this was the correct pace to give the villagers a good view of the bridal party. Through the village they went and then back again past the Chapel.

The rhythmic clip-clop of the horses trotting and the warm feeling of her husband sitting beside her added to Susan's feeling of happiness and fulfilment. The heat from his body warmed her, it was a feeling she never had before. Strangely she felt different, maybe she thought she felt married! It was only slightly less cold than it had been when it they set out for the chapel just over an hour earlier, yet Susan felt that it was ages ago and that the temperature had climbed. Charles's parents were not with them for the return journey because now, as a married couple they could be together without chaperones. Without chaperones, thought Susan, her worries about what was going to happen that night seemed to evaporate. Mrs Delaney was right, let nature take its course.

She was prepared for the coupling. God knows she had heard enough about that part, every married woman she knew sought to give her advice on the subject.
She knew it would hurt at least for the first time and she was ready for it. Mrs O'Brien would help her remove her outer garments and then withdraw. She couldn't bear the idea of taking off her underclothes in front of a man, like they were animals in the farmyard. She would put on her nightgown and lie in bed waiting for him.

Would she have a baby in nine months? Would she have a baby every year like the tenants and poor people did? She hoped not but that was in the hands of God, she supposed. Lost in such thoughts and somewhat oblivious to her new husband, the carriage made its way back to Kildangan House.

It was not until they were half way up the avenue to the house that the first drops of rain began to fall and Susan stopped the carriage and had the covers put up, but first of all, diplomatically and in line with her new role and status, asking her new husband it this was alright. It was the first time since her father's death that she had to ask a man's approval for something she wished to do and it annoyed her, but outwardly she smiled while thinking that this was just her new life and she would just have to get used to it.

III Postscript.

Kildangan House
Kildangan
Co. Kildare.

18th October 1853.

Mrs Alice Rowan,
Sancta Maria,
Athy,
Co. Kildare.

My darling wife,
It is with greatest sorrow that I have to announce to you the death of my patient, Mrs Charles More O'Ferrall in the small hours of this morning. Mrs More O'Ferrall gave birth to a healthy baby boy but the travails of childbirth proved too much for her mortal and frail life.

She died of sepsis which set in as soon as she gave birth and it is beyond my skill as a doctor to prevent or ameliorate this, as we know only too well. It remains amazing and mysterious to me that this condition strikes even more often in the well heated and comfortable bedrooms of the well-to-do as in the miserable hovels of the poor. May she rest in peace and may God's holy will be done. You will be gratified to know that the Parish Priest of Monasterevin, Mr Michael Ryan attended at her deathbed and having received the sacrament of Extreme Unction she died in full communion with our Holy Mother Church.

In consequence of this I will not be able to return home to Athy until Sunday evening as Mr More O'Ferrall prudently requires me to supervise the care of the infant in the hands of the wet nurse who has already assumed her duties.

Mr More O'Ferrall is joyous and relieved with the acquisition of a healthy son who will be heir to his estates and responsibilities.

His happiness, of course, is tempered by his grief at the loss of so dutiful a wife. You will remember that the estate and the village of Kildangan came into his hands by his fortuitous marriage to this gracious lady. The child is to be christened Dominick at the pre-arranged wish of his wife whose late brother and father bore the same name: a fitting and appropriate adjunct to this tragedy.

Mr More O'Ferrall has been kind enough to instruct his coachman to deliver this letter to you. I regret to inform you, my dear Alice, that the behaviour of the tenants, villagers of Kildangan and outside workers at the house has been nothing short of scandalous. Since the death of Mrs More O'Ferrall a great keen has gone up in the countryside all around, which as you know is customary among the peasantry. A great many of the countrywomen and their children have gathered outside the house. The insolence that I have received at their hands has been truly shocking. One woman verbally assaulted me with insults as to my professional capabilities. Some old widow woman, well known in the locality and called Mrs Delaney; half nurse and half witch was refused entry to the bedside of the late Mrs More O'Ferrall on my instructions and in consequence, the people blame this for the death of her Ladyship.

The ignorance of our Irish peasants sometimes makes me despair about their eventual betterment for which we all strive. So dominated by superstition and belief in fairies, spells and incantations, they refuse to accept the scientific advances of our modern world. It is a great tribute to out late leader Mr O'Connell that he was able to control and moderate their behaviour. Sadly his death in Genoa on his way to pay homage to his Holiness, our beloved Pope Pius IX left a void in public life that has as yet to be filled and I doubt if anyone of the calibre of Mr O'Connell will appear again in our generation.

The behaviour of the peasantry outside Kildangan House on the night of Mrs More O'Ferrall's death put me in mind of the antics of the Parisian mob leading to their murder of their late King and Queen. Thank God we live in a law abiding society. Please be assured of my safe return on Sunday evening at 7.00pm approx. Though I have been treated with the utmost of respect and granted every hospitality by Mr More O'Ferrall including dining at his own table, I miss comfort of my own fireside and your blessed company.

Your loving husband,

Thomas Roynane (Dr)

Chapter 3

Crimee Tommy

9th May 1854

His father had left him and three other lads from the estate to the barracks in Naas and walked in with them to the recruiting sergeant. After that it had been a gruff handshake and a goodbye between father and son. His father looked at him and his face reddened "When you are in foreign places, son, you stay away from dirty women" Tommy looked back, perplexed. What would he be doing near dirty women? Anyway, he was sure that the women in Turkey washed themselves, the same as the girls in Kildangan. He was going to ask his father what he meant but he saw how embarrassed he was, so he just replied "I will Daddy." This awkward exchange over, his father said "You'll have a fine pair of whiskers when I see you next" It was the older man's attempt at a joke as he knew how much Tommy wanted facial hair to show how grown-up he was. But he was yet to sprout the bushy locks that his father and all the grown-up men sported and that he admired so much. His father's bushy brown locks were the nicest of all and he longed to have ones like them.

Even as his father was speaking, it dawned on him that this was it, the leavetaking from his family and the move out of his own past life. Neither had showed any emotion at the parting but Tommy noticed that his father was looking away and not into his eyes and he could feel his sadness, his emotion. He knew that tears would come later as his father was that sort of man, he often cried over a sick horse or dying bird. Tommy knew that he too would cry when he thought of his family and of Kildangan. But that would come later for him too, alone to both of them. His mother had been bawling crying when he had left her early that morning at the door of their cottage in Kildangan. "That is the way of the world," his father had said and then "We rear them and then they go away."

Tommy was sure that her sadness would be wiped away and replaced with pride and tears of joy when her eldest son donned the Queen's colours and fought with bravery in the faraway lands of Turkey or even Russia itself and especially when he returned in his splendid uniform at the war's end, full of stories about adventures in strange places and maybe with a few bob in his pocket.

The whole country was in uproar with excitement over the war which was in a faraway country called The Crimea, though everyone in Kildangan called it The Crimee as they were unable to get their tongue around the last syllable. Nobody in Kildangan had ever heard of it, except of course Mr More O'Ferrall who had encouraged his tenants and workers to join in the war effort and guaranteeing them a place in his employ when they returned victorious. Well maybe the schoolmaster and priest knew about it as they were book learned too.

Tommy's only fear was that it would be over before he got there. The Russians were trying to take over Turkey by invading the Crimea country, Mr More O'Ferrall had said. This would disturb the peace of Europe and if they got away with it who knows where they would strike next? Maybe even India, they would hardly come as far away as Ireland though. They were a greedy, backward and rapacious nation and would only be stopped by brave lads like himself taking them on. He knew that his father approved and was even slightly jealous of the adventures ahead of him, but these were for young men like himself, not for old men like his father or Mr More O'Ferrall for that matter. He shivered with excitement at the prospects of sailing in a ship to far off Turkey or Russia or The Crimea and fighting in a strange land. He had never been on a ship, how exciting that would be? So different from the humdrum life in the stables of Mr More O'Ferral's estate in Kildangan where the highest position he would ever reach would be that of a groom and never see anything outside his own village and townland, except maybe as far as Athy or Monasterevin. He wanted to travel on a train too and see the world and he could never do that slaving away in Kildangan.

But, all the same, he liked his life at home and his work in the stables and he would return someday, when he was old and settled and seen the world. Then it would be nice to be a groom and settled down with a pretty wife and family like his father.

At night he would share the bed with his wife. Imagine sleeping every night with a girl! What would that be like? Would they ever stop riding? Doing it all night, every night until dawn and it was time to get up and go to work.

Tommy felt his mickey get hard at the idea, he would even skip this part of his life if he could get on to that part but he tried to put it out of his head and think of soldiering. That time would come and it would be the best, not like when he did it at the courtin' tree and his friends waiting to ask how it went.

Now though, he might become a hero in a great war and be the toast of all Kildare and even Ireland. He was even going to get paid for it! It was too good to be true. The Queen's shilling would give him a great start in life if he had enough sense to save some of it, as his father had explained.

The training was hard, rough and repetitive but Tommy had expected that. Mr More O'Ferrall had explained all this to him and to the other boys. It was to teach soldiers to obey orders, to make them a disciplined and effective fighting force, the best in the world and more than a match for the backward Russians. It was very exciting learning to use the carbine but the drilling was long and boring and he really could not see the point of it, in spite of what he had been told, he knew how to obey orders, sure everyone who worked in a farmyard knew how to obey orders, you wouldn't last long if you didn't. Marching like wooden soldiers all across the Parade Ground and back again and again, wheeling and turning to orders barked at them though, seemed pointless. Listening to the sergeant shouting orders abusing the young recruits was hard enough; not to mention his bad language that Tommy found rude and unnecessary, though he liked swearing himself, when his father wasn't around.

It made him seem more manly, but there was something in the sergeant's use of it that made it bullying and sometimes he felt like hitting him a smack but he knew that was out of the question if he wanted to stay in the army, not to talk of the punishment it might bring down on him. It was made quite clear early on that disobedience would be punished by a flogging and though he had never seen one, the boys had explained to him, quite graphically, what that entailed: the screaming in pain, the broken skin, the swish of the whip and the blood streaming down a boy's back. He could imagine the whiplash, every roar of pain, the blood dripping down the back in lines where the whip had opened the skin. No, he didn't want that and the boys could see the look of fear in his eyes and laughed out loud at his terror. "You take your punishment like a man" one of them had said "no place for cry babies in the army" and Tommy had nodded his head in agreement.

Even worse than the threat of flogging, was the food. It was brutal, how he longed for some of his mother's lovely bacon and cabbage. Sometimes they even had spuds and especially her apple tarts with a bit of cream on top. All the food in the army was cooked by men and you could tell: it was so rough and ready and the

kitchen workers all seemed to be disabled in one way or the other, some with limbs missing, some with wooden legs, some with only one arm. It seemed as if they were ordered to the kitchens when they were no use on the battlefield or the parade ground. He was fed up of bread which seemed to be the staple diet of soldiers, what was wrong with spuds, he wondered?
There was plenty of them in the country now that the potato blight was gone away and new breeds introduced.

He hoped that maybe the food would be better when he got to Russia or to wherever they would end up, though he knew that was stupid. How were they to get any grub at all in a foreign country? What country could feed an invading army? They would have to bring their food with them, how could they manage that, shiploads and shiploads would have to be brought halfway round the world.
This was a big worry to him and to the other boys, they talked about it incessantly. It was even more important than girls. It was bearable only because they knew that their days in the Curragh would soon come to an end and they would soon be off to the war with the other brave Irish lads to fight the Tsar's savage hordes of Cossacks and become heroes. Then they wouldn't have time to think about the grub or maybe not so much.

Just to think of the thrill of battle made him shiver with excitement, standing shoulder to shoulder with his Irish comrades, fighting the Russians and his comrades being killed and wounded all round him, but not as many as the Russians. Then they would charge the enemy and rout them, it was great stuff altogether. He also liked the company of the other fellows all around his own age from the four corners of Leinster, they were a great laugh, always joking and bantering with one another. The feeling of comradeship was a new and warm one that made him feel very grown up indeed. He knew he could depend on his new friends in the time to come as they could depend on him. He didn't feel lonely at all when he was with the lads.

He had would have loved to join the Hussars and ride into battle on a horse and wearing a gorgeous uniform but his father and Mr More O'Ferrall decided differently. A fellow from Kildare must join an Irish Regiment and show loyalty to his native place, he was a Kildangan man after all and it would be not be fitting to join an English regiment. They must all show that Kildare men were ready and anxious to play their part in the fight to come and anyway the Hussars were for sons of the gentry and were able to pay for their own horses which his father couldn't. They would look down on him for being the son of an estate worker and though he had always been taught that he was as good as any other man. He knew he was more comfortable with the foot soldiers who came from the same background as himself. So it was the 18th Royal Irish Regiment of Foot for him. All the same, they did have a great uniform, with a scarlet tunic and blue breeches with a red stripe running down the side
They even had a black head-dress called an Albert Shako with the regimental badge on it and a green ball tuft on top. What dashing fellows they looked! He

wished that they could see him in Kildangan dressed like this.

What a swagger he would make! Maybe he would be allowed wear his uniform home when he returned home from the wars.

Tomorrow they would leave for Dublin and take ship to Turkey, a steam ship going half way around the world to the Sultan of Turkey's country to protect it from the savage Russians. What a thrilling adventure!

An end to a long month of training would come the start of a life full of action.

What sights he would see, the like of which no Brennan had ever seen before!

On the night before they were to head into Dublin to board ship for the Crimea, many of the lads stayed up drinking from poteen they had smuggled into the barracks. There would be hell to pay if they were caught or maybe not as the ship to Turkey would have to be full, it could hardly wait until punishment was meted out. After a few scoops, with his head dizzy, Tommy lay on his bunk imagining what it would be like to go on a ship around the world and then into the thick of battle. He had heard that everyone on a ship got sick and vomited up everything in their stomach, good reason not to drink too much on the night before a voyage. His mind wandered due to a mix of excitement, anxiety and alcohol. He would have to kill Russians. What would that feel when he killed his first one? He supposed it would be just like killing a fox or a rabbit in a trap back home in the woods around Kildangan. The prospect excited him, it would be like hunting except that if he didn't shoot first he might be the victim, but that was war. Killing your enemy was fine in a war, not like when there was peace, funny, he thought, it must be hard for soldiers to stop killing their enemies when they got home from the fight.

At 6.00 am the following morning the troop train left Naas for Kingsbridge Station in Dublin. Tommy had never been on a train before though his father had taken him to see one a year earlier when they had first started to pass through Kildare. What a huge and powerful machine it was. All noise and smoke and iron and beautifully painted, what a marvel of engineering! Most of the lads were half drunk as they marched to the station but the sergeants and officers didn't seem to mind, it was as if they thought it was normal and expected behaviour.

The townspeople of Naas lined the streets and cheered, even at this early hour. What a lovely feeling that was, Tommy felt like a hero already.

Then into the station and on board the giant machine and it tugged and hissed and belched smoke as it headed off to Dublin through the green and fertile land of his native county. This was the way to travel, it was so speedy in comparison to walking, even running or a horse and cart, or even on horseback. Maybe a racehorse might outrun it but not for long! Tommy felt the thrill of speed made even more satisfying when he could see the fear in some of the other boys faces as they hurtled through the countryside. They must be moving by at least 20 miles an hour.

He was so proud of himself, his lovely uniform and the gallant lads with him, now at last he had that feeling that he never had before but had been waiting for. At last he was a man, he had never felt like this in the presence of his father and mother. His mother especially always treated him as if he were a child. He was a grown man now and a soldier. How great it was to be 15 and his whole life ahead of him. He thought of how proud his mother and father would be if they could see him now. At about this time, they would be rising from their featherbed in the newly build bedroom in their cottage in Kildangan, if only they could see him now, their eldest son as he headed off to the wars. But he knew they were thinking of him, maybe even praying for him.

It took them just two hours to reach the train station in Dublin called Kingsbridge, a beautiful new building on the banks of the River Liffey and just at the edge of Dublin City. Imagine, travelling so far in just two hours! Some of the lads felt dizzy and thought they might vomit over their new uniforms, the train had been moving so fast and they were so excited anyway, but all held their composure even if they felt otherwise. They, like Tommy had never been on a train before, but he loved the thrill of the high speed, though it did make him feel a bit dizzy. Shooting through the countryside and past the sleeping little houses and villages as if by magic, the train had left a huge plume of smoke in its wake like some fire-breathing monster. It definitely had been travelling well over twenty miles an hour some of the time.

When they descended from the train and got their feet on solid ground, the high spirits of the young soldiers continued and there was an outburst of singing and laughing which kept up all the way as they marched into Dublin.
It was a great thing indeed to be in the Queen's army.

At Kingsbridge Station there was a band to meet them from the nearby Royal Barracks. Marching music filled the air as the trainload disembarked and lined up to head into to Dublin City which was just half an hour's march away.
All along the route which was on the right bank of the Liffey, as they marched into Dublin there were small groups of bystanders to meet them and cheer them on, but they all knew and hoped it would be nothing like the crowds when they reached the centre of the city. Now in perfect formation and stepping together in their almost new uniforms and boots, led by the band, proud as peacocks, they knew and revelled in the impressive sight they made under the beaming sun and the admiration of the crowds.

The troop reached the spot where Parliament Street was at right angles to the river and they turned onto it. What a delightful shock awaited them. Here the whole population of Dublin City seemed to have turned out. The pavements were packed and people waved from the windows shouting encouragement and cheering wildly. The windows and shopfronts were hung with red, white and blue flags and bunting. Mixed with them were the emerald green flags of Ireland some with gold harps and shamrocks. Dizzy almost with the excitement of it all, the scarlet army turned left down Dame Street and past the statue of King William sitting watching them from his horse. Beautiful girls waved handkerchiefs and jumped up and down, their breasts heaving and shaking with sexual excitement, or so Tommy thought. There would be some rutting in Dublin town tonight, he imagined. As soon as it got dark every alleyway and lane would be full of couples at it hammer and tongs. The young men too had that wild sexual look in their eyes as they roared with excitement. Even the portly, heavy breasted matrons had that wild look of hunger for excitement and love in their eyes. God, it was great to be a soldier!

All the same, some of the lads would spill themselves before they reached the ship; the sexual nature of the parade, not to talk of the rough calico rubbing against their groins was too much for them. When they got to their ship they would be cooped up on board ship all night. Meanwhile all Dublin City would be carousing while they were playing with themselves or with one another.

The children jumped up and down with excitement and some ran the full course of the route to be with the marching host. At Trinity College they turned right and marched up Nassau Street heading for their next stop. It was to be the Westland Row Station where another train would take them to the port of Kingstown, twelve miles south of Dublin.

Two train journeys in the one day! At Kingstown there would be a ship to take them overseas to the war.

In the harbour at Kingstown sat the HMS Tyrone. It was a magnificent sight for Tommy and his follow recruits. They were overawed at its size and height. Its huge sails flapping in the breeze. If many had never been on a train till this day then none had ever been on a ship and had only dreamed of it.

Tommy, like most of the other boys, being from an inland county, had never even seen a ship before. The most these Leinster men had seen were small boats on their local rivers, but this ship was the size of a landlord's house plus its great barns and haggards put together. It was a miracle that it could even float. No wonder the crowds gathered around the quays were going wild with excitement. Yet there it was, a huge ship waiting for its cargo of Irish soldiers ready to sail half way round the world to teach the Tsar of Russia a lesson he would never forget.

A new band awaited them at the station and blazed up yet again for the short march from the station. The soldiers, still flushed with excitement were directed on board up a wide gangplank and didn't even have to break formation. They were the last to arrive, their provisions having been loaded the previous day as well as a troop from the 11th Hussars who had that had gone on board that morning. It was a cavalry regiment and its horses and forage had been loaded the previous night.

Tommy's only disappointment was that it was a sailing ship. He had hoped they would be on one of the new steamships, what a thrill that would be, but he supposed they were being used for the English soldiers. Afterall, England was even farther away from Turkey than

Ireland or so Master Brian Merriman, schoolmaster in Kildangan had explained to him. He had told them about the war in the Crimea, a country on the Black Sea, and that must be true as Master Merriman was the most learned man in the village even though he was a bit too fond of whiskey for his own good, his father always said. The Black Sea, whatever that was but it sounded so strange and exciting. A black sea, he wondered how that could be, maybe the rocks at the bottom of the sea were black making water seem black.

The ship smelled fresh and clean but Tommy knew that wouldn't last for long with hundreds of frisky young fellas sweating and farting. It would soon have that familiar and manly smell that he was accustomed to from the barracks. They were crowded into the hold and that was part of the fun, they were practically packed next to one another, like peas in a pod. Three men to a bunk and some in hammocks slung between the upright posts. They would have nothing to do all day except admire the sea. They wouldn't even have room for drilling and marching, thank God; himself and the other fellows were fed up with that.
They didn't have long to wait. At six that evening the tide was favourable and the HMS Tyrone lifted its anchors and in full sail headed out of Kingstown Harbour to the cheers of what had now swelled to thousands of onlookers who lined the quays. Gracefully and slowly the huge ship moved out into the open waters of the Irish Sea.
Tommy and his fellow soldiers were on their way.

It wasn't long before the novelty of sea travel wore off the young passengers on the HMS Tyrone. They were barely at sea for half an hour when Tommy felt a churning in his stomach. They hadn't eaten since early morning in the barracks at Naas and had grumbled at the lack of grub. Now he learned why. In the pit of his stomach he felt a pain growing each time the ship rocked, which was every few minutes. Soon his head ached and he felt dizzy and sick. He was standing on deck with two other lads from home. Now he felt his face grow pale and his belly heave. He could do nothing but try to bend over the side as he felt the vomit well up from inside him. Wiping his eyes, he saw his two friends throw up too.

Making matters worse was their inability to get the horrid, stinking stuff over the side and into the sea. Their lovely uniforms were going to be ruined. Feeling like death, Tommy had his first experience of seasickness. It was the worst thing he ever felt in his life. He thought he would die. The sweet, rotten taste inside his mouth, the dirt and smell of the stuff made it all seem worse.

But soon it was over and pale and shaken, he looked around. The whole deck seemed a throng of men getting sick, over the rails and on the wooden flooring. To make matters worse, the sailors were laughing at them and jeering them. "A lot of good you lot will do in Russia, you'll have to learn to aim that stuff at the Cossacks, it'll frighten them more than your guns." Some of the boys were angling for a fight with them but were dissuaded more be their own weak state then by the fear of the lash which they knew would inevitably follow a punch-up on board.

After awhile the vomiting stopped as the men had little left to throw up, but they hung around in small pale groups. Tommy was shaken and now felt very tired and weak. He wiped his mouth with his hand and lay against a spar. So this was life at sea, he thought, well they could keep it as far as he was concerned. He would never be a sailor.

Lying against the same spar was another soldier, dressed in a Hussar's uniform and smoking a pipe. "How are you bearing up, young fellow?" he asked. Tommy pulled himself together; he didn't want to let the side down by being seen as a weakling.

"I'm fine, never better in my life, its just that I amn't experienced to being at sea" he replied, a little bit too softly for his liking. "Don't worry about it" the older man replied, "Most lads get sick at sea at first, you'll soon get used to it".

Tommy eyed up his new acquaintance. He was much taller than him at about six foot two and had jet black curly hair, a huge moustache and a brown tanned face that showed him to be at least as old as twenty-one, which Tommy considered to be quite old. "Are you Irish?" he asked. "Yep, I'm from Dundalk, but I'm a cavalryman now and I'm probably from nowhere special, but I was born in Ireland and I suppose that makes me Irish for ever." "Of course it does" said Tommy, not really understanding what the man meant. "Have you always been in the cavalry?" he asked wide-eyed in admiration for this dashing soldier.

"Yep, joined at 13, had a great time, I'm a bugler see, I sound the orders, was taught it at home, you play the bugle?
"Naw" said Tommy now quite in awe of the man's accomplishments.
"They only play the fiddle round my parts or maybe a mouth organ." "And where might that be?"
"I'm from Kildare" replied Tommy; "a small place called Kildangan."
"Name?" "Tommy Brennan"
"I'm Billy Britain" the older man replied. "Bugler to the 17th Lancers, pleased to make your acquaintance, Tommy my boy" said his new friend rather condescendingly.
"I thought it was the 11th Hussars who were here with us."
"Your right, Tommy, it's a bit of a story but I'm to join my own regiment as soon as we reach Turkey, our commander is Lord Cardigan, who is yours?"
Tommy blushed with embarrassment, he didn't really know.
"Its General de Lacy from Wexford", he bluffed, he had heard that man's name mentioned among the boys.
"Here, do you want a drop of this, it'll settle your stomach?" Billy passed him a half-full bottle of rum and Tommy forced himself to take a swig of the horrible stuff that tasted like one of the Widow Delaney's cure-all bottles that he was given at home when his mother decided he was poorly.
Billy Britain was a bit of a drinker as Tommy learned over the next few days, but lots of hard men were. Maybe that was why he wasn't with his own regiment;

he might have gotten drunk and into trouble.

Each afternoon they chatted on deck and Billy regaled him with stories of life in the army. More often than not he had a rum bottle concealed under his jacket from which he swigged when no one was looking. Where he got it and the constant refills from, Tommy didn't know but he guessed it was better not to ask. He had little to tell Billy as his times in Kildangan seemed so uneventful in comparison to his new friend's. Billy had been at barracks all over England with the 17th Lancers and was often in trouble with his officers over his exploits. He knew lots of women and where to find them. They all loved men in the service, Billy assured him as Tommy blushed even though he knew that it was true. The stories became more exciting as the voyage progressed.

Soon they became the highlight of Tommy's day. Each morning Billy was busy foddering and grooming his horse as all the cavalrymen were. The foot soldiers' task were light, cleaning their kit and their quarters. Boredom and the horrid plain and dry food was their biggest complaint, so Tommy looked forward to his daily chat with his new friend. His friends from home were dull in comparison; they could only talk about things that Tommy knew about himself.

"Are you a man yet Tommy?" he asked.
"I suppose I am, I'm sixteen" he lied, "My daddy said you're a man at when you can do a day's work and I have been working in the estate yard since I was ten."
"Ah, Tommy my lad, that's not what I mean at all,

you're a man when your girl has a babby for you" said Billy. "In Kildangan, when your girl gets up the pole, you have to marry her, is it different in the army?" Tommy felt stupid and uncomfortable. "God I didn't know that, has your girl had a babby for you?" "Yep" said Billy nonchalantly sucking at his pipe "Several." Tommy looked Billy in the eye and saw a smile break over his face but he still didn't know whether to believe him or not. "Will there be girls like that in Turkey?" he asked. "Hundreds" replied Billy with a straight face.

"God" thought Tommy; "it won't be a bit like Kildangan" but he didn't say it aloud. "The only thing is that you have to be careful of the pox" Billy said in a measured tone. "What's that, is there a lot of smallpox in Turkey?", " Naw, its worse than that, it's a disease of the mickey, it breaks out in spots and poisonous stuff comes out of it and it hurts like hell" "Jesus, I wouldn't like that" said Tommy, now thoroughly alarmed. "You needn't worry" said Billy, you only get it from dirty women, tarts, women who expect to be paid for a ride" "Oh" said Tommy, then the penny dropped, so that's what his father was talking about when they said goodbye at Naas. He found it hard to imagine women who had to be paid for it though he had heard that there were some like that who hung around the Army Camp at the Curragh. "The girls in Kildangan aren't like that at all" he said. "They are more likely to hit you a smack on the head if you were slow about doing it with them" and Billy smiled at that. Then they both laughed. There was more to being in the army than fighting and drilling, thought Tommy.

At great speed the ship sailed south, down past the Bay of Biscay which always had to be avoided because of its treacherous currents and dangerous storms. The weather was choppy and strong gusts blew all the time, frightening the young lads from Leinster as they cruised south down the coast of Portugal. But it was exciting as well. In spite of the bluster they felt very safe with all their mates around them and in three weeks they had rounded the Spanish mainland and then docked at Gibraltar, which was an English port though it was in Spain, it had been taken from them in a war long ago. The Spanish couldn't like that too much, Tommy thought. He and his pals were really excited about the idea of getting onto dry land and exploring the place. It looked like a giant rock pushed up out of the sea; it would be fun to climb to the top. The harbour was full of ships of every sort but especially warships and transports travelling to and from Turkey. This was going to be a great war indeed. What country could stand against such so many mighty ships?

They were to be disappointed. Guards were mounted on the quays and nobody except some officers was allowed onshore. It was a lousy trick they all agreed. Billy explained that it was to stop them jumping ship and deserting. How the hell would they want to do that for and they hundreds of miles from home and not a word of Spanish between them? Anyway weren't they happy in the army?

"I suppose some of them might be feeling homesick for their Mammy's milk" was all that Billy would say to him after that, maybe he was feeling that way himself, homesick or whatever men feel when they are low even if they have no home. There was something sad about the way Billy said it. For the first time he felt sorry for his new friend. No matter what, he had his Mammy and Daddy, his brothers and sisters and his friends in Kildangan, they would always be there for him. Maybe Billy had no one: that would be a very strange and lonely feeling. Perhaps his mother was one of those women who hung around army camps looking for a few bob from a drunken, randy soldier or maybe even marry them.

He knew there was an army barracks in Dundalk, maybe that's how Billy came into the world. It must be hard to have no one to mind you. Where Tommy was from, even the poorest seasonal labourer who went around the county looking for work, had a family. Come to think of it, even the beggars had families. Now Billy was doing the same thing as his father had done: making babies without families. It was a funny old world alright.

After five days in Gibraltar, with fresh water and provisions on board they were off again. It was now unbearably hot and the sun blasted them out of it all day long. The ship started to stink even more with sweat and all sorts of body smells from the men and the horses in spite of the constant scrubbing it received. Everything was scrubbed except the people on the ship. The soldiers were smellier than the animals, they were lovingly groomed each morning, but the men...never. His mother wouldn't like that at all but he soon got used to it though he did try to keep himself as clean as possible, which was more than could be said for the other lads.

They were now in the Mediterranean Sea.

Tommy knew that the Pope lived in the city of Rome that was near this sea and from there ruled over all the Catholics in the world and that the great Daniel O'Connell had ordered that his heart would be sent there after his death to show his love for the Pope. Imagine cutting someone's heart out and putting it in a box and sending it to the Pope!

Well, that was The Liberator's wish and he was sure it was carried out with the best of intentions but he would prefer if his own heart was buried with the rest of him when his time came.

Also in the Mediterranean Sea was the island of Malta. Mr More O'Ferrall's uncle had once been the Governor there, his father had told him. At the far end of the sea was the Holy Land where Jesus was born and the Turkish Empire where they were heading. His head was dizzy with the adventure of it all and thinking of all the exotic places he was passing by. Slowly but surely thoughts of his home in Kildangan started to recede. He fancied he was getting like Billy now and that his place was here with the army and his comrades.

Their entry into the Bay at Valletta at Malta was splendid. Little boats owned by the Maltese came out to greet them. They were painted in bright colours: red and green and blue. Some were festooned with flags and banners; it was a great welcome. It was a grand sight and as they passed other ships a cheer went up and was answered loudly by the soldiers and sailors on the HMS Tyrone. It was very different to the entry into Gibraltar, which was quiet and dull. There might be some of the girls that Billy introduce him to in this lovely town.

As if he knew what he was thinking, Billy said, "A night out in a place like this would make a man out of you, Tommy my boy, these Malta women know how to give a soldier a good time and they drink wine like we drink milk at home."

Tommy didn't answer; he knew well what Billy meant and he didn't like the suggestion that he didn't know what to do with a woman, making him out to be a child. Sure every boy in Kildangan knew how to handle himself in that department.

Again they were to be disappointed, holed up in the bloody ship while the lovely city with its lights and white houses with red roofs tempted them like a devil from hell. They were frustrated beyond endurance, snapping at one another and threatening fights for little or no reason. What good was it sailing around the world if they weren't let off to kick up their heels every now and then, or even to do a bit of sightseeing?

He might as well be in Kildangan under the eyes of his father and mother. At least he would have the other lads to hang round with and an occasional trip to the Courtin' Tree. The bloody army was treating them as if they were children. It was alright for the officers; they were all dressed up in their finery and heading off for the town in carriages lined up on the quays.

It was better out at sea than stuck here imagining what it would be like to be on shore with plenty to drink and all those brown skinned women singing and dancing. The sooner they were out of this place the better.
In three days they were under sail again, heading for Constantinople, the capital city of Turkey where the Sultan lived. Jimmy Kennedy said that the Sultan had a thousand wives, one for every night in the year. When Tommy pointed out that there were only 365 days in the year. Jimmy conceded that he must have more than one a night or else they would unemployed but nobody really believed him. It sounded too outlandish.
The men on board ship were now sullen and depressed, they had been travelling for at least five weeks and it seemed like it would go on forever. They weren't even sure where they were headed, was it Turkey or Russia? After four days they headed into the Bosporus which was the strait on which Constantinople, the capital city of the Turk lay. It had once been a Christian city, he was told but was now the greatest Musselman city in the world. It seemed to go on for miles and at night they could smell it. It was a mixture of spices and dung, a dangerous but enticing looking place indeed. Its lights seemed to go on all along the coast. No chance of them stopping here, but it would have been exciting to get off and have a look all the same.
"The Turks are grave, haughty, courageous and faithful to their word, but sometimes cruel and revengeful" He knew this as the Schoolteacher Master Merriman had come to his house as soon as word got round that he was going to the war.

He has sat at their fireside and read the chapter "Parley tells about the Turks and about Turkey in Europe" from a book he had called "A grammar of modern Geography" by Peter Parley. It was a great story altogether and told the story of the wicked Sultan Bajazet who had kept another Sultan called Tamerlane locked up in a cage. It was great stuff and had held the whole family spellbound. But the Master had warned them that other parts of the book were very anti-Catholic and that was the only chapter he would read to them.

Billy was in top form though. "They say that the Turks do it with young men the same as they do it with the women"
"What do you mean, do what?" Tommy had innocently asked but he knew something dirty was coming. "Ride them" said Billy with a broad grin across his face. "How do they do that?" asked Tommy, knowing that he was being led up the garden path. "You'll know soon enough if one of those big, fat hairy Turks gets a hold of you." "Funny things you know Billy, did they ever do it to you?" asked Tommy and now it was his turn to smile. "Of course not" replied Billy "I'm not pretty enough, but you would be in with a good chance" and they both broke out laughing. "I bet you never heard of these things in Kildangan, Tommy Boy" said Billy. "You'd be surprised what we get up to in Kildangan on a summer's night" said Tommy, not going to let his own place be run down.
"In Dundalk we used to do it all the year round" said Billy who always wanted the last word.

On board, life continued with its boring monotony, its rotten smells and sickening food. In fact things seemed to get worse now as they approached their destination. The dried sweat of the hundreds of men on board mingled with the smell of their waste and the rotten food. It was amazing, thought Tommy who was used to dealing with horses, cattle and pigs in More O'Ferral's yard, how men smelled much more rancid and foul than animals did.

The boiling sun seemed to magnify the odours making the ship smell like a floating cesspit. It was now just a stinking shit-house. In Kildangan where they scrubbed themselves clean with rags, nobody at home smelled as foul as the officers and men aboard the HMS Tyrone, no not even the dirtiest beggar. They went on and on and into a new sea which they were told was the Black Sea. Tommy remembered the name and was looking forward to seeing it but with the other boys was more than a bit disappointed when it just seemed the same as the Mediterranean Sea.

A strange and mysterious name as there was nothing black about it at all.

Finally after about seven weeks of travelling the ship dropped anchor at a place they were told was called Varna. The countryside looked dusty and scraggly as though dried out by the unmerciful sun which beat down on it. Only a few bushes and withered grasses were visible from the shore. They must be half way between Turkey and Russia. There was no port and they were taken off the ship in boats. This was an adventure for the men but the poor horses suffered.

Cooped up for all their time at sea like birds in a cage, now they were lowered into the water and had to swim ashore. He could see the terror in their eyes as they kicked in panic when their hooves failed to touch the bottom. Many of the poor creatures just drowned. Yet it was amazing how almost all of them swam ashore. "If the men were treated like this they would all drown. A horse's instinct for survival is a great thing, much better than a man's" Billy told him as they stared in wonder at the horses swimming to shore. They cheered when each beast made it to the rocky beach.

Then it was time so say goodbye to his new friend who was off to join his 17th Lancers. He was the first friend Tommy had made away from home.
"We'll meet up for a few drinks as soon as things settle down, I might even get you one of those women" Billy promised with a broad smile that Tommy would always remember.
"What about the war, won't we be busy with the war?" Tommy asked, "There's no war here, Tommy my boy" the older man said, "Look around, we'll have to march off to find it". It was all beyond the boy from Kildare. They have sailed thousands of miles and now hadn't even been landed in the place where the war was, it was hard to understand. Tommy's unit assembled on the beach and soon they were marching inland. Here the countryside changed and soon lush meadows and orchards surrounded them. The fields were filled with multitudes of flowers and fruit bushes of kinds they had never seen before. The heat was unbearable and something they had never endured before in Ireland.

There was a huge lake was on their right and they saw in the distance the poor little town of Varna. Right into the countryside they marched carrying their heavy packs of supplies, a baggage train at their rear carried heavier supplies of food, tents, powder and shot, he supposed.

Their training now came into play as sweat drowned their faces and their legs and shoulders ached from their sudden exertion after their many weeks of enforced inactivity on board ship, they were now paying for their seaboard leisure. Yet they were all young men and well able for it and welcomed the physical toil as their sleeping muscles starting working again just like animals cooped up for the winter. Soon they got into the pace of the march, each man encouraging the other with his marching. They were now moving as a huge unit rather than a group of individuals. It was a welcome change to their previous five weeks of boredom. In the evening, some twelve miles inland they struck camp, their white tents making a little town of their own. The Russians were to the north, besieging a town called Silistria. Soon, maybe even tomorrow, they would march there and give those Rooskies a hammering. Each man was given half a mug of rum and some dried, crumbly bread which was called biscuits before bedtime, it was the same horrible grub that they had on board ship. Exhausted from the march, their muscles ached but they were in high good spirits. Tommy and his friends from Kildangan settled down for the night and slept like logs.

Billy Britain at bugle practice in the Phoenix Park.

Chapter 4

Into the Crimea

The camp near Varna was a hellhole. Tommy and his comrades couldn't figure out what there were doing there, just hanging around while there was a war being waged only a few miles away. They were going to miss all the fighting. It was like being in the barracks near Naas again except for the scorching sun. All day, sweating like horses they marched about doing parades and drills and wasting time and energy, just as if they were still back at the Curragh. All day the insects buzzed and bit. The countryside, which had looked so pleasant, was full of swarming insects, the worst were biting flies called mosquitoes. They were like the midges from home but much bigger and had a deadlier bite. They were nasty bloodsuckers. At night they attacked while the soldiers slept in their tents and each morning the soldiers were covered with lumps as big as halfpennies. They itched like hell and got worse the more they scratched and everyone scratched the lumps even though they knew that made them worse.

This was only a mild irritation in comparison to what was to come next. Within a few days some of the men started to come down with fever. It was the same sickness he had heard his parents talk about that had killed so many people during the famine time in Ireland. It was the dreaded cholera which the Irish boys feared more than anything else, it had killed the poor people in droves. They blamed it on the dirty water, rotten food and the scorching sun. There was always something to blame; in Ireland people blamed it on the dirt that was part of the lives of the poor. First came the vomiting and diarrhoea, then the men were in such a weak state that they could hardly leave their tents to use the latrines. This added the horrid stench of shite to the bunks where the sick were trying to shake off the dreaded disease. Hardly anyone seemed to recover from it as they sunk towards death in their own stinking mess. It was pitiful and terrifying to see. Oddly enough though, the Irish boys seemed to catch it less frequently than the English or Scottish lads. Maybe it's because we're more used to it in Ireland thought Tommy dolefully but that wasn't much of a consolation.

How rotten was it to travel so far for a war and to die of the fever even before you reached the battlefield? Watching men he knew sink towards death brought back his religion to him. No, he didn't pray that they might go to heaven but he asked God and his Mother to help them recover and especially that he wouldn't catch it or the other boys from Kildanagan or Billy Britain. He often wondered if he really believed that God would help the army so far away from home, but it was all he could do. The doctors seemed just as powerless as the sick themselves, there only cure was to keep the healthy men away from the sick ones, this was cruel as friendship seemed to give some consolation to dying men but it seemed to work a bit.
They all believed that you could catch it from a sick man even if he was your friend. In the scorching weather their uniforms itched and dug into their sweaty

bodies. Worse still the latrines were filled to overflowing and attracted thousands of flies and rats. The dirt and smell was everywhere. The water tasted horrible and the Irish lads avoided it as much as possible but it wasn't easy in the heat. They couldn't drink the rum all day, even if they had it or they might face a flogging if caught while drunk on parade. Now in late June and early July 1854 there was a stench of sickness all over the camp that never seemed to lift. It took until mid-July before the casualties started. Diarrhoea and unquenchable thirst were the first and in many cases the last signs among the men.

Then there was no cure, the soldiers just died off in their own shit and sweat. Some were carted off to the hospital in Varna but none seemed to return. They were not afraid of the enemy but all were terrified of the cholera. The medical orderlies could do little but alleviate the suffering with drinks and rest but only one in a hundred seemed to survive.

Only the priests could offer any hope. The Irish lads returned to their prayers believing no human agency could help them in the face of the fever. Only a move from this dreadful place where the disease seemed to come up out of the ground would save them.

They wanted to fight; at least then there would be a chance of surviving. Here there was no hope, just drilling in the baking sun and waiting for the fever to fell them. It was maddening entirely.

What could the generals be thinking of, leaving a whole army to die in this godforsaken place and not a shot fired in anger?

Still nothing happened, just more drilling and marching and the ever scorching sun. There was no move to Silistria to fight the Russians. The Light Brigade to which Billy belonged in his 17th Lancers had headed off, led by Lord Cardigan to find the Russians. They had returned exhausted almost 10 days later stumbling into camp, some half dead from heat and exhaustion, and no sight of the enemy. The Russians had left Silistria; they had been beaten back by the Turks, all on their own. Surely they would now be moved out of this dreadful place to somewhere that they could have a go at the Rooskies and escape the fever.

A real notion of dying in this place now confronted Tommy and his friends and they prayed fervently for safe exit out of Varna. Each night, half drunk on the increased rum rations they fell asleep hoping that the cholera would avoid them for another day. Each day and each night the stench of young men dying pervaded the camp. Tommy thought he could smell the fear of the Irish lads each night in their tent, though in the day they put a brave face on it. If they stayed here then the whole army would succumb. It was stupid beyond belief to shipped half way around the world to die of disease in this godforsaken place.

At last, when morale was on the ground the men were told they were to move. They were to take ship for the Crimea, which they were told, was right inside Russia. At last they would see some action.

They were to take one of the Tsar's principal fortresses, the small city and port called Sevastopol. That would teach him to stay away from Turkey or any other of her neighbours for that matter. The country around the fort was called the Crimea though it was ruled by Russia, just like Ireland was ruled by England. Tommy wondered what the Crimean people thought of that. Probably the same as the Irish thought about the English strutting around their own country. The relief of the men was immediate. The terror caused by the cholera lifted almost as if it had never been there. Action and excitement at last, and a new place far from this disease ridden plain, this was why they were in the army. Soon ordinary feelings returned to Tommy and the Kildangan lads. A great sense of excitement and optimism pervaded the camp. Soon the jokes were flying and as they packed their tents and headed off down the road to Varna, it was as if the nightmare of the previous two months had never taken place. Billy was off too with his fine cavalry unit and his nobleman general. He would get Tommy something to remember the Crimea by, he said as he bid farewell to his friend, then gave him a lecherous wink. Russia was a wild place and they would have the time of their lives. "As if he knew anything about Russia" Tommy thought but as usual just kept his mouth shut as he promised to look up Billy when they settled into their new camp right inside the Russians' own country. But he was delighted with Billy's good humour and sense of fun.

On the 8th September 1854 the Royal Irish Regiment embarked at Varna for the Crimea. It was a great relief to be on board ship again and heading for a new country. They were invading Russia! Sailing along the Black Sea coast again was a thrilling adventure and not like a hardship at all. Funny name the Black Sea, for this beautiful blue ocean thought Tommy yet again, there was nothing black about it at all. Names were strange things though, maybe "black" meant something else in whatever language they spoke around here, Russian maybe.

The transport ships were each towed by a steamship and that was a thrill in itself, the power of these steamers was amazing, being able to pull a huge ship! What would they invent next?

Warships flanked the whole convoy to protect it against any Russian attack but no one expected that to happen. What navy could withstand the might of such modern ships? These Rooskies would regret the day they took on the Queen's Navy. It was a magnificent sight, moving at speed through the tranquil sea.

The gentle lapping of the waves against their transport vessel, the absence of drilling and most of all the fact that they had left the dreaded cholera behind them, lifted the spirits of the soldiers.

They could live like this for awhile.

After just a week at sea they reached their destination where they were joined by the Army of France which was an ally in this war. Everyone was against the Russians it seemed. Their emperor was an absolute monarch called the Tsar, Mr Merriman had said. This meant that they didn't even have a parliament or elections, not that that mattered much to the boys from Kildanagan. Only people who owned property had a vote. But this was more proof that they were on the side of right; everyone was ganging up on the bully. A bully to his own people as well.

The landing place was a beautiful, scenic spot called Calamita Bay or "Calamity Bay" as the boys soon called it. Tommy, not used to the sea found it fascinating and a bit scary, the lapping water, ebbing and flowing seemed dangerous to a man who couldn't swim but he kept his fear from the other boys though he supposed most of them felt the same. He was sure none of them could swim either. Strangely, it was deserted, no one to meet them and shoot them out of the water. Neither was there a house or cabin nor a soul around as far as the eye could see. It was about thirty-three miles up the coast from the city and fortress of Sevastopol. Soon after landing they would march to the city through open country parallel to the seashore with the ships of the Navy moving along the coast to protect them. It was a great plan; army and navy working together. The Russian army would then try to block their way and destroy them into the bargain. That would be the Russians first battle with them and for sure it would be the last for some poor unfortunates on both sides.

Maybe then, when the enemy discovered what they were up against they would break off and the war would end, that would be a pity. The soldiers would fight them on land and the ships would bombard them from the water. Exciting times ahead!

They had expected the fierce horse soldiers of the Tsar; the Cossacks, would be there to attack them as they landed, surely they would protect their own country and stop a hostile army from landing on their shores? But no, they were quite alone, that didn't make sense but they were grateful to be able to land safely as they would be very vulnerable as they disembarked from the ships. Anyway, Billy had said that the Cossacks rode ponies and not horses, Tommy wasn't sure if this was a bit of a joke, he couldn't imagine fierce soldiers riding ponies, that would look a bit silly but nevertheless they would have been sitting ducks if they were attacked as they came out of the water.

Later on in the day some lads had spotted horsemen on the hill behind the beach, but not a shot was fired at them as they landed right in the Tsar's back yard. It seemed as if the Russians were saving themselves for a fight later on. It was a strange way to behave, Tommy thought and the Irish lads agreed with him. If they had been attacked as they disembarked, the casualties would have been huge, maybe they would all have been slaughtered on the seashore and the whole operation abandoned.

But no, the enemy had stayed away. If this was the way the Russians thought they could defend their country then they would be easily defeated. When the army reformed, with their supplies and heavy guns they would be unstoppable. If it was going to be as easy as this then they would capture Sevastopol in a few days and be heading back to Ireland before Christmas!

This was a lovely country alright in the beautiful Crimean autumn, and the ease of their landing gave the soldiers a great lift in spirits. There was no road and marching across country was going to be like a ramble in the fields back home. In great form they assembled in their units and spread out on the beach. Here they had to spend the night without cover. Their tents had not been unloaded. The boys were grumbling again and later on it rained. Not a soft Irish rain but a heavy downpour.

In the morning they shivered in the weak sunlight. Feeling miserable and their uniforms soaked through, they cursed the stupid officer who had ordered the loading of their tents first of all, so that they could not unloaded until all other cargo had been embarked.
"I hope they remembered to bring some stores," Jimmy Dunne had said with his voice full of irony. Their stomachs were rumbling from hunger and they feared that no food was at hand, not even a dry crumbly biscuit.
"Some of these bloody officers shouldn't be let out without their Nannies." Jimmy was the blacksmith's son from Kildangan and he had no respect for the gentry. But they had breakfast alright: by some miracle, the food stores had been unloaded. They waited around all day for the rest of the army to come ashore.
The officers were surprisingly lax with them that day: A sure sign that at long last they would see some action soon. Tommy was even able to meet up with his friend Billy Britain who disembarked that morning with his horse and the 17th Lancers. He was in cheery and smiley as ever and, like all of them, spoiling for the fight to come. Finally on the following day, the order they had all been waiting for was given.
They were marching to Sevastopol!

The territory through which they marched was hot and dry but still smelled of countryside and greenery; it was almost like home except for the heat and the lack of trees and ditches. In the distance they could see the ruins of burned out farms. The Cossacks were out there alright making sure that there were little or no supplies left for the invading army. It was a tiring march but undertaken in good form by the high spirited troops. They went for full ten miles before they reached their first obstacle. It was a middling sized river called the Bulganek, about the same size as the River Liffey which they passed on the way into Dublin city. It was going right across their paths. Lo and behold, what was on the other bank but the Russians waiting for them? Smiles spread across the ranks as everyone chattered with delight, a fight at last!

They cheered as the cavalry crossed the river and headed towards the Russians on the other bank. Tommy waved frantically as he saw Billy Britain ride proudly, trumpet in hand, beside his commander Lord Cardigan. What a splendid sight it all was, magnificent horses with gallantly dressed riders! It looked like one huge animal moving towards the enemy rather than hundreds of individual horsemen. The bright navy blue-jacketed and trousered riders, stripe down the side of their leg and mortarboard caps making them seem even taller in their saddles. These were the brave men of the 17th Lancers. How terrifying and proud they looked as they forded the River Bulganek and headed towards the enemy. The footsoldiers waited on the near bank for the Russians to be driven back by the brave cavalry before they would be ordered across to clean up the rout and no doubt capture some fleeing Russian soldiers, maybe even their stores. Disappointingly, the Russians pulled back as the cavalry led by Lord Cardigan crossed the river. This was looking too easy. As the Russians retreated, the horsemen followed and were soon out of sight over the crest of the hill.

The men could see Lord Lucan, the overall cavalry commander follow. The Irish did not like him, he was a rack-renting landlord from Mayo and everyone knew him by reputation as greedy and heartless. It was even said that he had evicted tenants during the Famine when many were in arrears all over the country. He had let them die of hunger and disease on the roadside or forced those who could afford it, to emigrate.

After some time the sound of musket and canon fire was heard from the other bank. That would be our men giving the old Rooskies the first taste of battle. But they were to be disappointed; only about a quarter of an hour later; the cavalry re-appeared and much to the shock of the infantry and the rest of the army started to file back across the river. They were running away from the Russians. When the truth dawned on the men on the riverbank they started to jeer the retreating cavalry. Shouts of "Yellow, yellow" and "Cowardly bastards" rang out.

The horsemen were furious and sat upright in their mounts, staring straight ahead. Tommy knew that they had been ordered back, so it wasn't their fault really so he didn't join in the jeering. Then he saw Billy Britain, still at the side of Lord Cardigan, and he blushed to the roots for his friend. Their eyes met for a fleeting moment and he could see the shame and embarrassment in Billy's countenance. Nobody jeered at the officers of course, that would have brought down a flogging on the offender, but the message was clear even to the high-and-mighty gentry on their mounts; the cavalry was in disgrace. There would be no battle today. The army camped for the night on the banks of the Bulganek River. Maybe tomorrow the shame of the army in running away from its first engagement could be erased. But the Russians were gone too; maybe they would make their stand farther on down the coast. Then there would be a mighty battle. As Tommy settled down for the night he hoped that Billy would join him for a pipe. They would share stories over a smoke and have a laugh. There was no sign of the Dundalk man that night; he must be reeling under the shame of the cavalry's retreat.

The next day they were on the march again. No doubt the Russians were waiting for them somewhere further down the coast on the way to Sevastopol. The next river they had to cross was called the Alma and when they reached this about mid-day; sure enough the Russians were waiting for them. It was a great relief for the soldiers; at last the marching and drilling was over. Here was a battle. Even before they reached the river the Russian artillery opened up. Tommy felt a thrill in his spine. They were going in to fight.
They knew what to do, just shoot as many of the enemy as they could and march through them, so this was it, this was the war. He was going to kill a few Russians! He felt the excitement race through his body. With the boys from Kildangan on either side and the massed soldiers in their red jackets stretching for hundreds of

yards on each side, they halted before the river waiting eagerly for the order to advance. The French army was to take the area between them and the sea; they were further inland and in a continuing line. The whole front would move, in a co-coordinated way, delivering blow after blow to the Russian army.

The French moved first and the British army had to stand their ground in perfect formation waiting for their orders.

Meanwhile the Russian artillery opened up them in earnest. The roundshot came whizzing through their ranks. The soldiers knew they must hold firm and in formation in spite of this. They could see the shot coming and flinched to avoid it while the officers roared at them to remain in line. This was hard to do as their natural instinct was to duck or shift as they saw they oncoming shot but the line held, in spite of the butchery caused by the canon. Men roaring with pain and terror as they were torn limb from limb by the iron balls which they could see coming towards them. Most men just fell to the ground in silence. Tommy didn't know what he would do if he saw a shot coming for him. He felt the roof of his mouth go dry with fear. He ground his teeth and stared straight ahead. Then it was over. In spite of the gunfire they heard what they had been waiting for.

Clear and welcome the bugles sounded "advance" and a loud roar of delight burst through the ranks that the Russians must surely hear. In a dead straight line they marched ahead, their rifles and the outstretched swords of the officers gleaming. It was like a huge red wave moving towards the river.

It felt very reassuring and safe to be surrounded by other soldiers as they moved. Again and again the Russian artillery started to take effect and gaps began to appear in the lines even before they reached the river. Then the moaning and shouting started as men fell, their bodies pierced by shot and shrapnel, some of them with limbs blown away completely. The screams of pain, the thud, thud noise of the big guns firing at them and the smoke in the distance. They had not as yet fired their guns and the Russians were cutting them up really badly. On they marched, heads fixed to the front, eyes staring ahead in a mad stare, that way they did not see their fallen comrades but they could soon smell the powder and the smoke hurt their eyes as it drifted towards them. But they could hear their comrades alright as they screamed in agony.

They headed to the riverbank, then straight into the water. It only came up to their waists and they held their guns over their heads.

They kept their formation as they advanced through the now muddy waters of the River Alma. There was a bit of red in it too and Tommy knew what that was. Soon they were out the other side, keeping the straight line of their formation. The artillery was still pounding them. These Russians sure were expert gunners and were changing their range to rain down hell and death on the oncoming troops as they advanced slowly but steadily towards them. They must have hundreds of big guns to make such an impact. As yet there no rifle fire that was in range to hurt them. Tommy was beginning to sweat now. Even though he knew he shouldn't, he looked around and found one of his Kildangan friends had gone missing. He was Jody Henry, the shoemaker's son. Now he shivered, the boy must have been hit. He felt terror just for a moment but then it left him as he moved on without thinking.

His head was pounding and his mouth had gone all dry. Now his legs were beginning to stiffen with terror but his instinct kicked in and told him to stay with his troop, there was safety with the others, safety in numbers. Staring straight on, a rhyme came into his head. It was an old nonsense thing his mother had taught him called "Brian O'Lynn had no shirt to put on" and now it kept going round and round in his head:

> "Brian O'Lynn had no britches to wear
> So he got an old sheepskin to make him a pair
> With the fleshy side out and the woolly side in,
> "They'll be pleasant and cool" said Brian O'Lynn."

He tried to find the rest of the verses in his head and kept marching on with the line. It seemed as if all the other soldiers were in a trance too as they marched together as one, through the shot and smoke. Straight ahead they heard the booming of the big guns, louder now, but it didn't effect the line that marched on, directly on and shoulder to shoulder.

> "Brian O'Lynn though his house had no door
> Had the sky for a roof and the earth for a floor.
> He had a way out and he had a way in
> "Tis a fine habitation" said Brian O'Lynn"

Across the river there were low hills; up there was the Russian army waiting for them. That's what they were advancing towards and they kept marching on. Now more and more gaps appeared in their ranks as the canon found its range again and again. Each time a gap was formed, the men moved in and closed it.

> "Brian O'Lynn, his wife and wife's mother,
> Were all going home o'er the bridge together,
> The bridge it broke down and they all tumbled in,
> "We'll go home by water" said Brian O'Lynn"

Without flinching they reached the ridge and found the enemy gathered around their big guns. At last they were able to use their new firearms. Shooting wildly now they aimed into the masses of Russians. Their new guns, called Minie Rifles with a range of 500 yards had a deadly effect. These were the latest in modern technology. They were breech loaders which made them quicker unlike their enemies guns which had to loaded through the muzzle and so were much slower and had a shorter range. The smoke was dense now and choking. As the Russians fired back they soon realised that they were out of range. Their old muskets just didn't have the range of the new ones of their opponents. It was like shooting at boys using slingshots. The Russians fell in heaps round their canons. The fire was constant now as the Russians were mown down. Line after line advanced pouring the killing shots into the massed Russians. By the time their own old fashioned guns were in range they were surrounded by heaps of their dying soldiers. As the army marched towards the canon the Russians began to fall back. At first slowly but soon they began to run. They left their poor screaming comrades in their hundreds on the ground behind to suffer and die. As they ran they dropped their guns and kit bags, some even threw off their greatcoats as they ran to speed themselves up. Tommy kept moving on. Now he had to walk over or on the dying and dead Russian soldiers. He didn't like that, he tried to avoid that but couldn't all the time. Now his incantation of Brian O'Lynn was replaced with "God have mercy on them"

It was sickening to see but he knew that he was safer now and that they were winning the battle. All around were what seemed to be thousands of screaming and dying Russians and hundreds of his own comrades. Tommy tried not to look at them but even so he could smell blood mixed with the bitter stench of canon and rifle fire. The army marched on, clearing everything in front of them. Then after only for about a hundred yards more they were ordered to halt. They remained there in case the enemy regrouped and returned but they all believed that there was little chance of that. The cavalry would finish off the fleeing Russians and drive them all the way to the gates of Sevastopol, maybe even inside it for safety and shelter. Billy Britain would have his chance to see some action at last.
It was a great victory. For the second time that day a great cheer broke out from the ranks. They had smashed the enemy and won their first great battle of the war.

Behind the still ranked soldiers the Medical Orderlies were removing the sick and dying. Tommy stood beside Jimmy Dunne."What happened to Jody Henry?" he asked. Jimmy replied "He was hit even before we got into the water, poor bastard." "Is he dead?" Tommy asked sheepishly. "How the hell do I know?" answered Jimmy and stared madly at him. Tommy looked around, the other soldiers near him had that same mad glare in their eyes. That's from killing Tommy thought, that's what it makes men look like. He could feel his own heart jump in his chest as if he wanted to go on and kill more. That's what it was, a mad rush to the head, they had all gone a bit mad from the battle and the killing. Later they were given the task of digging pits for the dead of both sides. Digging was bad enough in the warm sun after the battle but tossing the corpses into the pit was the worst of all. It was a horrible job especially as many came across the mutilated corpses of friends or acquaintances. Most of the bodies were still warm. Luckily Jody was not amongst them. He must have been one of the wounded that were taken to camps behind the lines before being loaded onto the ships and taken back to Turkey to the military hospital at Scutari near Constantinople. Tommy prayed that the boy would be alright and come back to them or better still, to be sent back home, he was beginning to think that if a man had the bad luck to be wounded in his first battle, then he wouldn't have much chance of surviving the war. Luck had a lot to do with this business.

That night they camped on the ridge they had taken

from the Russians. Their pots were full and they were given extra meat and rum rations to celebrate their victory. But there was a strange feeling of unease amongst them. In spite of the carnage and terror it seemed as if it had been too easy, too quick. It seemed as if they wanted more fighting, more killing and more blood.
Tommy could feel the tension and knew that the slightest remark could lead to a fight, the men were still so wound up, running and jumping around the place and raising their voices when they spoke. He was surprised and didn't like it that Jimmy Dunne was still acting strangely. The men had tasted blood and wanted more. He could feel it, it was all around, it was like the smell of sex, it was all around the camp that night. What strange dangerous creatures men were when surrounded by death and bloodshed, and loving it. They were really like hunting animals, like wolves, he thought. Billy came to visit him that night. The 17th Lancers were camped nearby. They had not been allowed to chase the fleeing Russians.

"The Officers are livid and so are the men" Billy confided. "They were running away, we would have cut them to pieces,Captain Nolan is saying terrible things about Lord Raglan, it's a bad situation." "Who the hell is Captain Nolan anyway, does he think he knows more than Lord Raglan? I'm sure Lord Raglan knows what he is doing" Tommy replied, and though he sounded deferential he also believed it.
"The officers don't think so" said Billy, "they think he is a bungling old fool and afraid of taking a risk.

Captain Nolan is not like most of them, he isn't even gentry. He wrote a book about cavalry tactics so he knows what he's talking about." "What good is a book about war, sure that's not a story at all?" asked Tommy amazed that a book could exist on such a topic. "Sure Lord Raglan is as brave as a lion, he even fought at Waterloo where he had his arm blown off." "That was years ago and he was young then. Why didn't he let us charge the Russians when they were running away, we could have slaughtered them? " Tommy remained quiet, thinking that it wasn't only the foot soldiers who wanted more killing, Billy was that way too. The Russians had run away, that was a victory, what more did they want? But he didn't say that as he saw that Billy was losing his temper, totally worked up: his face red and his eyes staring. He was as crazed up as the men in his own company. They sat in silence and pulled on their pipes. "You'll see plenty of action yet, Billy, my man, don't you worry, anyway where are all the girls you promised me?" Tommy knew he had lowered the tension when Billy smiled and cuffed his friend jokingly on the shoulder.

But for the first time since he left home, Tommy felt alone, he did not share the bloodthirsty feelings of his fellow soldiers. He had hoped that Billy would feel the same as him, but no, he was just like the others. Tommy, in the middle of a huge army, felt all alone.

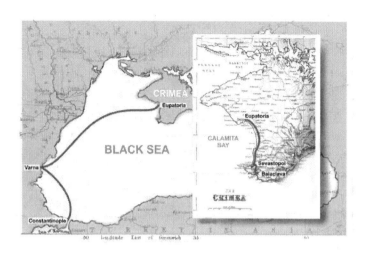

Map showing battlefield sites and Tommy's route to the Crimea.

Chapter 5

Outside Sevastopol.

Tommy would remember that night after the Battle of the Alma for the rest of his life. It was his first taste of action as a soldier. Sure it was a great victory. The horrible suffering: the moans of the wounded and the dying, the smell of the dead and the exhaustion that he felt seared into his memory, never to be erased. The bloodlust of his comrades amazed and disturbed him and then the loneliness he felt when he realised that none of his friends felt as he did. Buoyed up by the excitement of the battle, the men found it hard to sleep in spite of their exhaustion and the extra rations of rum that were doled out. They had done a lot to clear the wounded from the field and they had had to bury the dead. They were dumped into pits with no name or record to mark their resting place. The bodies of the officers were treated differently, they were taken to the rear, identified and given individual graves In some cases their bodies were sent home. It was the same in death as in life, he thought, officers and gentlemen were separated from the ordinary folk. All around them that night they heard the screams of the maimed and the dying. From across the river where many of the wounded had been moved there was a constant cry. Calls of men begging for aid, calling for a drink of water, shouting on God or Mary to help them, filled the night air. Most heartrending of all was the sobbing moan of the boys who called for their Mammies to help them.

Their pleas were mainly in vain and by morning there was silence from the wounded. They were silenced forever.

The sawbones were in action too; the surgeons were amputating the limbs of the wounded right here on the battlefield. The dreadful Russian artillery barrage had shattered thousands of bones and limbs. Now these must be cut off the living to save their lives and the cuts and wounds cauterised. If this was not done quickly then the dreaded gangrene would set in and this would mean certain death with the flesh and bone rotting on their shattered limbs and stinking into the bargain. They were held down by the medical orderlies or sometimes by their own comrades and dowsed with whiskey or rum to ease the pain as the surgeons set about their gruesome lifesaving work. As thy cut through flesh and bone the sounds of the young soldiers screaming and moaning filled the air. Thankfully they couldn't hear the sound of the saws as they severed limb from body. Because of the tricks of the imagination, or maybe because of the terror they felt, the sounds of all this suffering often seemed to be closer still as their minds magnified the screams. Men shouted or moaned prayers or cursed and then went silent. Only the strongest or those with no feeling at all, seemed unmoved by the sounds of suffering, or maybe they had learned to block it out. It was a terrible thing to suffer and die out here in the middle of nowhere, far from family and loved ones.

Only daylight brought some ease as the men were

roused to bury the remaining dead and those who had passed away during the night, which were many. They also had to dispose of the amputated limbs, tossing them carelessly into the pits atop the bodies of the dead. The battle itself had been exciting, they had never experienced such a thrill as they marched man-to-man, shot and conquered. It was better than anything so far in their lives but now the anti-climax and the horror of the dead and dying hit them right in their guts.

There was a price to be paid for everything and this was the high price for the thrill of battle. There was nothing for it except to put the head down and work till the sweat and tiredness emptied the mind of all thoughts and emotions. They spent all day digging pits for the dead and throwing in their comrades and the limbs of so many wounded. It was a gruesome and stomach retching thing at first to carry a dead man and dump him in the open pits. Touching his cold skin was worst of all but by the end of the first hour they were all used to it. Tommy learned to carry the corpses without touching the skin, he grabbed them feet first, leaving the other man to lift the upper portion of the body where he was more likely to come in contact with the head or gaping wound. Soon it felt they might as well be burying dead animals, they thought so little about it or at least that's they way they all behaved even if they were crying on the inside, Tommy thought.

The bloody work continued right through the next day. By now burying men who had died of wounds since the fight was their main work.

Two days after the battle the army was on the march

again. Sevastopol was only a few miles away and surely they would take it by the end of the week. They crossed two more rivers, the Katcha and the Belbec and the Russians were nowhere to be seen. At the Belbec, the horses that had not been watered since the Alma plunged into the water eager to slake their thirst. Lord Lucan sat on the other bank and roared at the troopers that he would flog any of them who allowed their horses to drink. He was a cruel bastard as the Irish knew and now the English lads got the message as well. This was uncalled for. Taking it out on the dumb beasts was a real sign of a coward, as all who had worked with animals knew.

The horsemen, shocked at the cruelty of their commander had great difficulty in getting their thirsty nags across the river without drinking from it.

Then like an apparition, there it was. The beautiful city of Sevastopol, down in the valley below them. Its gleaming white spires and buildings surrounding the harbour full of tall ships. Afterall the marching through the countryside the appearance of the city was something like a dream, it was so bright and shimmery. It was a gorgeous sight for the advancing army as the late autumn sunlight caught the whiteness of the town and seemed to light it up. A cry rang out through the ranks. "Hurrah for Sevastopol" and "Hurrah for Lord Raglan", some of the Irish boys even shouted "Erin go bragh."

Tommy smiled and felt the thrill of being part of all this, the horror of the Battle of the Alma now receding. The remains of the Russian army was inside waiting for them so it was no surprise to Tommy when they were

ordered to march around the city to its other side where an attack might not be expected though he couldn't imagine how the Russians wouldn't spot this.
The other soldiers had different ideas however and grumbled that they were not allowed to march straight in and take the city before the Russians had time to improve its defences. More bloody marching on an empty stomach but maybe Lord Raglan and the higher-ups knew best. They were to march around the city to the southern side and take the small port of Balaclava into which supplies could be landed from the ships. With fresh with supplies of powder, shot and grub, they would be even more formidable and the outgoing ships could take away the wounded . Then the attack could begin in earnest.
The army moved through the wooded landscape in a manoeuvre to encircle the city of Sevastopol. It was a boring and routine march and the only excitement was when the cavalry captured the Russians baggage train at a place called Mackenzies Farm, funny name, they thought, there must be Scots people here, fancy that, in the middle of The Crimea! The baggage train was at the rear of the Russian army, which was now marching out of the city, or so it seemed. This was very confusing, the men were ready and anxious to fight but the generals only wanted to move around each other's armies like dancers doing a polka. The British and French armies who were supposed to be attacking Sevastopol were marching around it and the Russian army which was supposed to be defending it was marching away from it. It was a strange way to conduct a war. Jimmy Dunne said that the Russian generals

were as much afraid of a fight as the English ones.

Billy came around in the evening with two bottles of French wine called champagne, looted from the captured Russian baggage train which he shared with Tommy and Jimmy. Tommy had heard of it alright, it was the favourite wine of the gentry and they guzzled buckets of it up in Kildangan House when they entertained their neighbours which was often. It was bubbly and lukewarm and didn't taste like proper drink at all. But it had an effect and soon they were laughing their heads of at the least thing. The new drink went very well with the rum which they had in good supply and they sat around the fire, smoking their pipes, bantering and chatting with the other men gathered around. Billy, always up for a laugh also had some ladies underdrawers which were also looted from the Russians officers' baggage. They had never seen anything like them before. The women in Kildangan didn't wear anything under their dresses except petticoats as they all knew quite well but Billy assured them of the nature of the clothes and they fell around the place laughing. Billy even tried one on for a laugh. They couldn't figure out what ladies' underdrawers were doing in the Russian officers baggage and Billy told them that there must be loads of whores in Sevastopol. Maybe they were intended as presents! Only women like that would wear such garments.

How Tommy admired his friend that night beside the campfire and how proud he was of him! His big head of black curls, the dark skin of his laughing face shining in the firelight, his playful brown eyes and his long, slender legs spread apart so manfully. It seemed as if he had never seen so handsome a man. All cavalrymen had skinny legs he had noticed, that's because they were on their horses all day and didn't get to use them, not like the foot soldiers. Billy's infectious laugh and the smile he radiated made everyone around him happy, that was a magic gift that some men had. Tommy hadn't felt like this since his last night at the Courtin' Tree, he could see Billy looking at him in the same way too and that the other boys sensed what was going on, especially when they saw how red and flushed his face had become and how fidgety he was, moving his hands all over his body and shifting in his stool as if he could never become comfortable. So what? All the soldiers who had a chance were doing it and the officers too, he would bet. It was not as if there were any girls around anyway. He would make his move when Billy headed back to his own camp. There were plenty of shrubs all around where they could get some privacy.

Billy was in an excitable mood and just chaffing for action. He told them that all the cavalrymen felt the same, especially Captain Nolan. The Russian army was heading north and would attack when it was good and ready; maybe then they might have some real fighting. Their commander was Lord Cardigan who was in charge of the Light Cavalry Brigade and over him was that rascal Lord Lucan.
Even though these men were brothers-in-law, they weren't on speaking terms. That didn't bode well, Billy thought. The cavalry and the men had little respect for

either of them. Especially despised was Lord Lucan whose cowardly behaviour at the River Katcha was still discussed. According to Captain Nolan, these noblemen had bought their way into their commands and that was why they didn't know their arse from their elbow when it came to fighting. He called Lord Lucan "Lord Look-on" for his slowness in taking on the Russians. He said that Lord Raglan himself was a doddery old fool; he had fought at the Battle of Waterloo in 1815, way before any of them were born, and was far too old and too slow to be in charge of a modern war. He didn't seem to have the stomach for it either or the whole army wouldn't be sitting on their backsides outside of a city they were supposed to take.

On their way around Sevastopol, the infantry stopped at a small, poor hamlet called Kadikoi to the south of city. It was made of mud walled huts with roofs thatched with reeds, so different from the neat houses and villages of Kildare. The cavalry then marched on and took Balaclava, which was a fishing village nearby, much more prosperous looking than Kadikoi and with its own small harbour. There was no battle, Billy told them about it later; they just marched in and took over. There was no Russian resistance at all.

It was a godsend to the navy who would now able to use it to land supplies and the whole area would soon be turned into a vast military depot. This was a serious war confided Billy, nothing was being left to chance. They were going to build up overwhelming numbers of heavy guns and modern firepower even if they mightn't be able to match the Russians with manpower. When they attacked Sevastopol it would crumble under the might of the guns being landed at the small port. Still there was the threat of the Russian army which had escaped and was now to their east, they must be re-grouping for a fresh attack.

They would hardly let their city fall without another battle. Even when it did fall, they would be still knocking around, looking for revenge maybe. Afterall it was their country. Just one night in Kadikoi and then they were off again. This time they headed for Sevastopol itself. It was the 27 September 1854, hardly a week since they had landed in The Crimea. Once more they looked down on the lovely city, this time from the other side. It seemed to be surrounded from here by a wall that looked only like a park wall surrounding a big house back in Ireland, and yet they did not attack. The soldiers were perplexed. They could easily walk through and into the city; the wall was even broken in places. Tommy was beginning to think that there might be something in Jimmy Dunne's words; maybe the generals were stupid or cowardly or both.

They sat there for nearly three weeks without a shot being fired until the big guns were drawn up from the ships in Balaclava harbour. Meanwhile the Russians were raising mighty defensive forts, earthworks and walls all around the city. The soldiers shrugged their shoulders. At least the siege would start soon and their enormous guns would batter down anything the Russians would put up. There was no doubt about it; they would be victorious and heading home by Christmas.

The infantry moved to within range of the city's defences which were now being frantically and expertly strengthened by the Russians. It was very frustrating to see the huge earthworks and forts being thrown up while the British and French armies watched in idleness. The boys would get enough killing here; unfortunately it might be themselves who would be the victims. This was wrong, they shouldn't be delaying the attack, thought Tommy even if he knew it would all change when the batteries arrived and hopefully blew the defences of the city apart. So much could have been gained by an early advance but that opportunity was lost now.

There was nothing the men could do about it, Lord Raglan would decide, but the grumbling continued and something changed in the relationship between the men and their commanders in these few days. Even the junior officers felt the same, Billy told them that, but Tommy thought it was them who were stirring it all up. For the first time he felt let down by the higher-ups. They seemed blind to the obvious that even the roughest and most stupid soldier could see. Sitting outside the walls of Sevastopol till the Russians had reinforced it was a recipe for slaughter in the weeks to come and a siege that might well go on and on right into the winter. So much for a return to Ireland by Christmas!

They dug in just outside the walls, making their own earthworks and trenches, almost a mirror image of what the defenders of Sevastopol were doing not so far away, except for the forts that the Russians were building:

they were getting ready for the inevitable attack while the Allies were digging to protect themselves from artillery fire. The enemy forts would be hard to take. The Russians wouldn't dare come out of their city and attack them. They burrowed into the ground, for all the world like an army of rabbits. Each section then took position and waited and waited.

They could see the Russians quite clearly as they went about their work and sometimes could hear them talk and laugh and still not a shot was fired. The Russian army didn't seem afraid of what was to come at all. When the Allied soldiers were relieved of their duties for a rest, they marched back to camp where the boredom and monotony was worse even than the backbreaking work of building earthen defences.

The situation at Balaclava Port was disastrous. Due to incompetence and bad planning, ships were waiting outside the harbour, unable to unload their supplies. Meanwhile the soldiers inland were dying of hunger and malnutrition. Most disgracefully of all, wounded soldiers were dying in droves on the surrounding hills as there were no ships to take them to the hospital at Scutari in Constantinople. It took almost a year to rectify the situation and only then after a press campaign from home. When supplies at last started to get through, at least they could now look forward to a hot meal and a rum ration. The food however was rotten as ever, that hard bread and dry meat, but at least it filled their bellies. This was more than the poor buggers inside the city could expect, they must be starving by now or soon would be, eating rats and dogs or maybe nothing at all.

They had been cut off from supplies for weeks now and there must be thousands of men in there, not to talk of the ordinary inhabitants of the city. If they had any sense at all they would surrender.

There was booze too in the dugouts and earthworks. Sometime the lads would be blind drunk especially on the night watch when they were not so well supervised by their sergeants. Jimmy Dunne had come a cropper on this when he took up a dare from the other soldiers. Of course they were all a bit jarred on the night watch. They were spoofing about the way neither the Russians nor the Allies were shooting at one another.
"They'll soon shoot if we move out of our places," one of them had said. "They will in their arses" Jimmy had said, "haven't they run away from battle every time?" "One step out of the trenches and its you who'll get his arse blown off" was the reply while the other boys guffawed with drunken laughter.
"Right" said Jimmy and without another word dropped his rifle and sprang out of the trench towards the Russian line.
"Come back you mad bollocks," shouted Tommy after him but to no avail.
Jimmy ran to within gunshot range of the Russian line and dropped his trousers and turned his posterior to face the enemy. There was wild cheering from his own side. "Take a shot at that you yellow Rooskies" he roared and they did.
A few shots rang out in the night as Jimmy hitched up his trousers and skipped back to his own ranks amid the roars of laughter and clapping from his comrades.

He was put on a charge immediately and marched back to camp. The next morning the brigade was assembled and the charge and the punishment were read out. The unfortunate Kildangan man had been sentenced to twenty lashes. A leather whip would be used with nine thongs, it was called The Cat O' Nine Tails... a cruel joke.

The drummer beat a roll and the men stood to attention as the punishment was meted out. A doctor felt Jimmy's pulse and then nodded to the Sergeant that the man was in a fit condition to receive his lashing. Jimmy's shirt had been removed so that he could receive the lashing on his uncovered back and feel the pain more acutely and at the same time save his shirt from damage. The whipping was performed by the drummer of the regiment, part of whose duty this was. Tommy winced as the whip cut into the bare back of his friend and soon the blood trickled down.

The lashes were administered in a left/right line to avoid causing the soldier a heart attack. Jimmy's face froze from the brutal pain as the cat raised welts, separated one layer of skin from the other and after the second lash drew blood but he didn't cry out and Tommy was proud of his friend for that. After three lashes the skin began to peel from his back and though Jimmy's face remained expressionless, Tommy could see the pain in his eyes. It was callous and cruel treatment and yet Jimmy showed no emotion and above all, did not cry out. He would not give his tormentors that satisfaction. But Tommy knew what Jimmy was like. He was never going to forget or forgive this for the

rest of his life and neither should he.
The twenty lashes seem to take ages even to the onlookers who remained silent and stony faced throughout. The punishment was intended as much for them as it was for the unfortunate soldier, it was to teach them to obey orders and regulations no matter what. After the flogging Jimmy was checked and dressed by the medical orderly and sent back to join his comrades. He was a bit of a hero for a time afterwards to the lads but the stupidity and cruelty of the whole thing made Tommy feel sick and dazed. He could see now that the officers in the army had a cruel streak in them. This was no way to treat men, worse than animals, in fact no Christian would treat a dumb animal this way. It was cowardly and inhuman.

Finally the big guns were in place. They had been pulled and dragged from the ships in Balaclava harbour by mules, horses and manpower. What a sight they were even without firing! A line that stretched all along the south side of the city, as far as the eye could see. Their huge muzzles pointed at the fortifications and the city. These were no ordinary guns firing iron cannonballs. These were the latest invention. They fired exploding shells that would reduce the Russian defences to smithereens and terrify their army and the inhabitants of the city.
By the 17th October they were ready and the bombardment commenced. The men had never heard anything like it before. The deafening roar terrified them at first. Firing in groups so that the smoke would not hamper their aim these monsters lifted off the

ground when they shells were discharged and they spat fire from their muzzles as they discharged their ordinance. Then came the crash as the shells hit the defences of Sevastopol, blasting walls, stone and earth high into the air. How could anything or anybody withstand such a bombardment?

Back in camp many of the men and not only the gunners, were deaf for periods of time. The noise of the guns was so tremendous that it wrecked their hearing but they seemed to recover after a few hours away from the firing. Soon they learned to cover their ears when the discharge took place but it didn't seem to matter much, some of them were never to recover their full hearing. At first the Russian batteries replied but they soon fell silent, knocked out by the accuracy of the Allied guns. All day the bombardment continued till the soldiers thought the gun muzzles would melt and they really did get hot, burning the hands of any of the gunners, unfortunate and inexperienced enough to touch them. On the second day there was a massive explosion behind the Allied lines, a French magazine had exploded causing great causalities. The officers had no sympathy for them saying that it was their own fault for smoking and lighting fires in the vicinity of high explosives.

In spite of their allied status, the officers looked down on the French as being some sort of inferior force, calling them Frenchies and sometimes Frogs which was even worse. It seemed as if the ancient animosity between the two nations was a real as ever. The officers considered the French to be amateurish and a bit cowardly, preferring their showy uniforms to their guns and horses, not like the British Army, which was more professional. This attitude seeped down to the men and the two armies didn't mix except at the higher level. Communication would have been impossible anyway, as neither spoke the others language.

By now, most of the gunners suffered from constant headaches and some of the boys started to bleed from their ears.

Still the bombardment continued, right through the second day and the third. Then on the 20th of October as suddenly as it started the guns went silent. The smoke cleared completely for the first time in three days and the men got ready for an assault on the now ruined defences and the hopefully demoralised Russian defenders. Looking out they were amazed to see the Russians manning what was left of the city's walls and swarming over the few earthworks which were still intact.

Even worse, the huge Russian forts of the Malakov and the Redan, which faced the British lines, seemed in perfect working order and fired a few shots at the British lines just to show their defiance and that they were still in business. Three days of bombardment and so little to show for it! Why the hell hadn't they attacked a month earlier when the Russians were unprepared? With heavy hearts the men looked across at the enemy lines. If they were asked to attack now they would be cut to ribbons.

Chapter 6

Into the valley of death

25th October 1854

Half a league, half a league,
Half a league onward,
All in the valley of Death
Rode the six hundred.
Forward the Light Brigade!
Charge for the guns! He said.
Into the valley of Death
Rode the six hundred.

From " The Charge of the Light Brigade" by Alfred, Lord Tennyson

Billy Britain shuddered with excitement and he could feel the hair on the back of his neck tingle and rise; he knew that the great day had come. There had been fighting all morning as the Russian Army sought to break through the Allies' lines and take back the port of Balaclava. That would have been a great victory for them as it would cut the Allies off from their supplies and without replacement food and munitions they would be unable to sustain their campaign and the siege of Sevastopol. Billy was the Duty Trumpeter this week for Lord Cardigan. What a piece of luck! He would be beside his commander sounding out his orders when they went into action, as he knew they would and soon too.

This would be the day Billy boy! He had been in the army since he was thirteen and now at twenty-one he still had not been in a real battle. It was a far cry from his native Dundalk. Today would be the day of glory! Billy looked down the North Valley from where the Light Brigade was positioned. On the left of the valley was the Fedioukine Heights and on the right were the Causeway Heights, both of which had been taken by the Russians earlier that morning along with their batteries of guns. The poor Turks who had defended them had been routed and slaughtered by far greater numbers. The cavalrymen were dismounted and in the far distance. About a mile away he could see the faint specks at the end of the valley, which was the place where the Russians had placed their own artillery pieces. This made a U-shaped deployment of the Russian army with the Light Brigade holding the mouth of the U.

On the right hand side of the Light Brigade stood the Heavy Brigade, also dismounted and waiting for orders. To their left stood the gallant French cavalry, so beautiful and colourful to look at and at the same time, quite terrifying, a perfect military combination. The fighting had been heavy already that morning as the Russians had tried to break through, moving down from the Causeway Heights but had been held by the 93rd Highlanders and the Turks. It had been a desperate engagement as the thin red line of the Highlanders, only two deep had held back a cavalry force twice their size. It was a great achievement for an infantry troop to hold back a cavalry charge but these Scotsmen were no ordinary soldiers. They were tough mountain men who loved a fight. Defeat here would have been ruinous as behind them lay the port of Balaclava which would surely have fallen to the Russians had they not been held back. The Russians had retreated to the end of the valley behind their guns, leaving enough troops and gunners to man the captured cannons.

Lord Cardigan was with the men he commanded in the Light Brigade; as usual he had spent the night on his yacht, the Dryad, which he had brought from England. It was a great stain on his reputation that he should spend the war in such luxury while his men, even the officers, spent their nights under canvass on the hard, cold ground.

Even Lord Lucan, who was much more unpopular with the men, didn't display such a weakness for comfort and privilege, but then of course he didn't own a yacht. Unlike his men he sat mounted on his charger a bit back from where the Light Brigade was stationed at the mouth of the North Valley. As the overall cavalry commander he was awaiting orders from his superior Lord Raglan who was behind them all on the Sapoune Heights where he had a good view of the whole battlefield.

With him was the usual entourage and hangers-on: his staff officers and couriers, the Times correspondent William Russell who was another Irishman, and an officer's wife Fanny Duberley who was intent on seeing the whole war firsthand. She was nicknamed "The Vulture" because of her morbid fascination with battle. There also was the brave Captain Louis Nolan who was so critical of the conduct of the war by his superior officers. Like Billy, he too was just bursting for a fight especially one involving his beloved cavalry.

Up here on the Sapoune Heights, old Lord Raglan became deeply worried about the idea that the Russians were about to carry away the guns mounted on the hills on either side of the valley which they had captured that morning. It was considered a great shame to have guns captured by the enemy. Earlier he had sent an order to Lord Lucan to ride up the hills and prevent this. But Lucan thought that he should wait for promised infantry support which had not yet arrived.

The charge of the Light Brigade

In increased agitation Lord Raglan looked on as nothing happened on the valley floor and he could see clearly that Lucan's cavalry were dismounted. Meanwhile the Russians might well be leaving with the guns which though captured from the Turks were British made guns. It was infuriating that Lucan did not attack in spite of his order to do so. Now totally exasperated, Raglan sent another order to Lucan to get him moving. "Lord Raglan wishes the cavalry to advance rapidly to the front. Follow the enemy and try to prevent the enemy from carrying away the guns, troop horse artillery may accompany, French cavalry is on your left - immediate". It was dictated to and signed by General Airey who read it back to Raglan.

When Raglan's own Aide de Camp advanced to deliver the order Raglan said "No, give it to Nolan" knowing that Nolan was the better horseman and more likely to reach Lord Lucan first.

As Captain Nolan turned his horse Lord Raglan shouted at him "Tell Lord Lucan to attack immediately." Nolan's heart beat wildly, at last an attack and he dashed off with the thrilling order and a smile on his face.

Meanwhile down on the valley floor the men were having a quick respite from what they knew would be a hard fight. Some had taken the opportunity to have a smoke as much to warm themselves in the cold morning air as to steady their nerves.

Lieutenant Colonel Shewell was incensed and called on Sergeant Pickworth to take their names, only to find another Sergeant about to light up. Lord George Paget had just cut a fine cigar and regulation or no regulation was not about to throw it away, once cut a cigar must be smoked promptly or the flavour will suffer. Other officers were passing hip flasks containing whisky or

brandy around. It was standard eve of battle behaviour. The horses snorted and jingled their harnesses as if they too knew something was up. Billy Britain refrained from lighting his pipe though he would dearly have loved to. He would not dare risk a reprimand from Lord Cardigan who was nearby. There were some disadvantages to being Duty Trumpeter but he was not going to lose a pipeful of tobacco if asked to extinguish it when it was lit up. Worse still he was up till late drinking and carousing with Tommy Brennan and the other Irish lads and had only a few hours sleep before he was in his saddle again at 6.00am.
That seemed like ages ago but it wouldn't be long now before the Light Brigade was in action. He could feel it.

Lord Cardigan was cool as a cucumber himself, looking towards the ridges where the Russians held the British guns. He was in full dress uniform and he cut a fine figure in his gold braid, bearskin hat, cherry red trousers and handlebar moustache. He certainly looked the part of a dashing cavalry commander thought Billy. Though unable to see the guns from the angle of the valley floor he confidently expected an order to advance up there and retrieve them. It would be a good day's sport. Meanwhile Captain Louis Nolan dashed down the heights from Lord Raglan's position at breakneck speed. Though the drop into the valley floor was precipitous it was no problem for this expert horseman and his mount. This was the moment he had waited for: a cavalry charge that would prove all his theories about tactics. He drew his horse up sharply in the middle of the Heavy Brigade.

"Where's Lord Lucan? he shouted at Captain Morris. "Over there" his old comrade pointed. Galloping up to Lucan he thrust the note at him barely concealing his glee at having his superior at a disadvantage.
"Orders from Lord Raglan that the cavalry are to attack immediately." Lucan barely concealed his contempt for this disrespectful upstart officer. He read the note, then in obvious puzzlement re-read it. "Attack?" he asked. "Attack what? What guns Sir? Where and what to do?" Nolan pointed at the guns at the far end of the valley and not to the guns on the heights on either side and to Lucan's obvious astonishment said, " There my Lord, there are the guns. There is your enemy"

Lucan, much perplexed at the stupidity of an order to charge down the entire length of the valley in face of such terrific odds rode over to his hated brother-in-law. "Lord Cardigan, you are to attack the Russians in the valley" without looking him in the eye, Cardigan replied "Certainly, my lord". Then, as he realised the import of the order, he stared his adversary straight in the face and said, "May I point out that there is a battery in front, a battery on each flank and that the ground is covered by Russian riflemen?"
"I cannot help it" replied Lucan sharply.
"It is Lord Raglan's positive order that the Light Brigade is to attack the enemy." It was the longest conversation the two had since the war began and probably our last thought Lucan as he rode off to arrange the deployments for the attack.
The men now knew what was afoot when lines of battle were ordered.

Billy who had never been in a cavalry charge before was one of the last to cop it, but he knew it meant trouble the way Lord Cardigan started to snap at the men. It was unlike the old gent, though he was always frosty and distant he was normally courtesy and manners itself. The older hands were soon in the know; the Light Brigade was to attack the enemy guns full frontally, not only that but under the range of the guns manned by the Russians on each side of the valley through which they must ride and their riflemen too. Then they must head into the enemy's canon and the whole Russian army was probably behind them. It was madness. They would all be wiped out.

The 17th Lancers were to lead the charge. Their 9 foot ash lances with steel tips were known to terrify the enemy when held in the "down" position during a charge and they were lethal. Billy lined up with his comrades beside Lord Cardigan who would personally lead the charge. All voices were stilled now except for those of the officers who were barking their orders. Next came the 11th Hussars, the peacocks of the British army with their tight cherry red trousers, which got so much derision from the Times newspaper and so much admiration from the ladies. Their vanity knew no bounds: officers even wore whalebone corsets to keep their perfect figures; it was Lord Cardigan's own regiment. Lord George Paget's Light Dragoon's were to follow. At least their commander had a good smoke before the battle and he felt better for it. When the Light Brigade had led off, Lord Lucan would follow up with the Heavy Brigade which would give a knockout punch to the Russian Artillery. That is if they ever reached it, thought Lucan. Lord Cardigan, leading from the front accepted the fact that he might die like the rest of his troops, and he was the last of his line, like many officers in the Hussars, he had no children.

At ten minutes past eleven Billy heard the command they had all been waiting for, the order to sound "Walk." Lord Cardigan stared glassily ahead and led his chestnut thoroughbred "Ronald" in front of the 17th Lancers. The bugle call was echoed by the regimental trumpeters and like a huge and beautiful blue and red animal the Light Brigade's horses walked into the valley at the regulation speed of four miles per hour. Little noise was made at this speed, only the soft trod of the horses' hooves, more like a rumble than a thud accompanied by the jingle of their harnesses. Some horses snorted, perhaps they sensed the ordeal to come. Being intelligent beasts, all the horses knew this was a big event. As soon as the first line was clear Cardigan gave the order to increase speed to "Trot" which was eight miles per hour. They rode through a ploughed field making just a little more noise on the soft ground but as soon as they were out of it, the trod of the horse hooves on the hard ground made the threatening thud that indicated a cavalry advance. Now the pounding of the horses' hooves echoed throughout the valley. Billy could feel the intensity of the men's concentration as they moved as one into the valley, indeed he was part of it: the personalities of all the men merged into one. Lord Lucan now led out his Heavy Brigade. The bulk of the cavalry of the British Army in the Crimea was now heading for the Russian guns at the far end of the valley. What was later to be called the Charge of the Light Brigade was about to begin. Beyond the ploughed field the artillery, earlier captured by the Russians from the Turks on the surrounding hills, opened up. Now the boom of the guns, the smoke from their pieces and the smell of gunpowder began to fill the valley.

The Russian gunners on the hills could not believe their luck as the horsemen below them were completely at their mercy All the time they would spend going up the valley, they would be under the range of their guns. They would remain so till they reached the range of the guns at the end of the valley. So the horsemen would be under constant fire. They had walked into an obvious trap. The thrill Billy and his comrades felt soon changed to a daze as they realised they were riding through a deadly hail that would blow arms, legs, torsos and even their horses apart. At first it was a booming sound as the guns discharged, trying to find out their range. Then the thudding sound came as the balls ripped through the horsemen or bounced harmlessy on the ground nearby. More deadly though was the exploding shot which annihilated all underneath it if it went off at the right moment over the horsemens' heads or amongst them. Captain Nolan had attached himself to the 17th Lancers though he should have returned to Lord Raglan's command position to report back. But he wasn't going to lose this moment of glory. Just as the ride began and the firing started he rode to the front of the line and started to gesticulate wildly. No one broke line or paid any attention to him; they all had their orders and weren't going to deviate from them. Nolan had no authority here and they knew that he shouldn't even be with them. Billy gave him a fleeting glance and thought he must be a little mad riding about like that, he had no business being here. Then it happened, almost before the battle had begun.

One of the first Russian shells to be fired exploded about 20 yards ahead of the column. Right in front of their eyes a fragment pierced Captain Nolan's chest and he screamed in agony, but only for a short while, more in shock and surprise than in agony. Then he let go of his reins, the horse sensing loss of control by the rider turned and headed for home, she had had enough of this escapade. Nolan's lifeless body was flung to the ground. Nobody looked down as they rode past his bloody corpse. Their concentration was so great that that this first horror seemed not to affect them at all.

Up the hill Lord Raglan stared on in disbelief. What the hell was Cardigan doing heading for the Russian guns at the end of the valley when he was ordered to attack the ones on the heights on either side of it? The whole damned cavalry would be wiped out. As the mass of red that indicated the Heavy Brigade started to move off in silence he gasped, "Oh my God" in the forlorn hope that somewhere up the valley the horsemen would wheel around and ascend the hills, to take the recently captured guns instead of riding straight into the Russian guns at the end of the valley and certain disaster.

The French General beside Raglan said to him "This is magnificent but it is not war". Raglan turned and stared icily at him. The Times correspondent, William Russell continued to scribble frantically on his pad. This would make superb copy when it reached London. He was witnessing a live battle and his report would bring it to every reader in Britain and in time to the whole empire. From Caithness to Calcutta, men would marvel at the bravery of the Light Brigade and the recklessness of their commanders who sent them on such a dangerous adventure. How the bosoms of the ladies would heave when they read about the gallant horsemen who rode into the valley that morning!

By now the scale of the impending disaster was obvious to all. The French cavalry who had been on the left of the Light Brigade before the charge now moved up the hill in front of them. Under cover of some shrubs they moved against the Russian gunners who were pouring their shot into the valley below. With only muskets to defend them they hadn't a chance. As soon as they saw the French advance they knew that their position could not be held but they managed to hitch up some of the captured guns and take them with them as they fled. At least now, the deadly cannonade from the hills on the left of the valley had been silenced.

Lucan led the Heavy Brigade right into the valley through the pelting shot. Almost immediately he was wounded slightly in the leg. Though it was only a flesh wound where a bullet had grazed it, it drew blood. Then his horse was hit but not seriously either.

Riderless horses and wounded and maimed men from the first wave passed through their ranks, causing shock and distress to the advancing cavalrymen, yet they trotted on. Then suddenly Lucan had enough. He ordered his trumpeter William Joy to sound "Retreat."

Lucan turned to Lord William Paulet and said, "They have sacrificed the Light Brigade. They shall not have the Heavy, if I can help it."

General Scarlett, behind Lucan, did not agree. When he saw the advance guard turn around he countermanded Lucan's order and had his trumpeter to sound the "Advance". Lucan rode up to him and demanded he change the order. The men, both officers and troopers were horrified, not only was their honour to be compromised but the Light brigade was to be condemned to be slaughtered. Without follow-up support that might save them or at least reduce their casualties, they hadn't a chance. But Lucan insisted and had his way. After only minutes in the field, the Heavy Brigade returned to their starting-base at the end of the valley.

Billy rode on, keeping in the first line as near to Lord Cardigan as he could. As men and horses were blown apart the ranks closed making a solid line which would hit the enemy and their guns a deadly blow, that is, if they ever reached the guns. As soon as they left the range of the canons, now firing on them only from the hills on the right, the guns in front of them, those stationed at the end of the valley, opened up with deadly effect. Terrifyingly the riders could see the roundshot coming at them but could only move slightly in their saddles to avoid them. It was so strange and frightening looking at the great round balls approaching. They could see them clearly. It was like staring death in the face, if only for an instant.

They could not move their mounts from side to side, as

their knees were all just the regulation six inches away from the neighbouring lancer and anyway their training had taught them that the strength of a cavalry charge depended to a great extent on the solidity of the line of charge. Men were blown apart and dismembered body parts were flung at great speeds into other horsemen causing havoc, death and terror. Each time the smoke cleared they knew another round was coming, only seconds after the last. In perfect co-ordination the Cossack gunners fired together to achieve maximum effect. These gunners were more expert than the ones on the hills and they also had a clearer view and easier trajectory to aim at the oncoming charge. The men and horses of the Light Brigade were falling by the score. Shells were also exploding overhead while the roundshot was ploughing into their ranks but still the line held.

All about them, men with arms, legs even heads blown off were falling from their horses. Body parts were flung into adjoining horsemen, often with fatal results, worse was the splattering blood which dripped down their faces into their eyes and they could smell it as well. The brave horses being lower down got the worst and blew apart when hit by the roundshot. Some exploded like bursting balloons, their blood and guts covering the ground below them and a horrible stink rising from their entrails. Some escaped when their riders were killed or fell off. As soon as this happened, the confused horses generally turned and raced back to the starting line, as their instinct for the safety of home took over. When it seemed like hell itself was raining down on The Light Brigade a more deadly shot came from the Cossack guns. The roundshot was now replaced by canister shot, which spewed hundreds of deadly balls right into the charging cavalry.

They were now within eyeball distance of the Russian guns. Just then Cardigan roared at Billy "Sound the Charge". Billy held the bugle up to his lips and blew with all his might. The men, judging the distance themselves even without the bugle call lowered their lances to the level position and at 40 to 50 yards increased their speed to charge which was the fastest speed of their horses could make. Now with eyes bulging and lances lowered they charged the guns. Already some gunners were fleeing in terror as the might of Light Brigade fell on them. Some discharged a last round of canister shot with murderous effect. A roar went up from the horsemen as they slammed into the guns and the gun crews, spearing all on foot with their deadly lances. Just as he approached a gun, it discharged and Lord Cardigan disappeared in the cloud of smoke.

As the Dragoons and Hussars arrived at the guns a terrible revenge was already being enacted on the gunners who had earlier caused such slaughter. Those who sought safety in flight were speared in the back and those who remained were cut down in the heat and bloodlust of battle. The Lancers continued on, meeting the Russian cavalry whom they charged and dispersed. But then realising their huge superiority in numbers, the Russians regrouped and lined up, forcing the Light Brigade back to the gun line. From here, realising that the arrival of Lucan and the Heavy Brigade just wasn't

going to happen the troopers turned for home. They would have to fight their way through a barrage from the hills and the Russian cavalry now assembled to finish them off.
The Light Brigade would now be pushed back and maybe destroyed completely in the process. But they had done it: they had reached the guns and destroyed many of them. They had achieved what few even among themselves had thought possible, but there was no time to exult. Now they had to get back, anyway they weren't thinking now, they were working on pure instinct, acting out their orders and training.

The fighting on the way back was bloody and disorganised. The men now knew their lives depended on escaping the pursuing Russian horsemen and like butchers they hacked and stabbed their way through. Unhorsed men grabbed stray mounts and joined the flight. At last, after only minutes, which seemed liked hours, the few struggled back to the British lines at the end of the valley. They were a pathetic, ragged and bloody band but some managed a smile as they approached Lord Lucan's Heavy Brigade, sitting on their mounts as if the last half-hour hadn't happened. Their smiles froze as they were cheered by the brigade which had let them down by not following them into battle. Of about 650 men who took part in the charge only 175 mounted men returned. Those unscathed were sent back to their nearby camp and soon the surgeons started their bloody work on the surviving wounded. Gunshots rang out as the wounded horses were put down.

Thirty year old Corporal James Nunnerly, mounted on his brown mare, with tears streaming down his blood spattered face, rode in and gently handed the limp body of Billy Britain over to the orderlies.

He had carried him in his arms all the way from the Russian guns at the far end of the valley and then cradled his lanky frame as they approached the British lines. Billy still had his beloved trumpet strung around his shoulders. It was pierced from a Cossack sword but Billy had held onto it for dear life. James Nunnerly was able to cough out "Take good care of this brave boy". He returned alone to his tent. He had shared it with nine others, all had left in high spirits that morning but he was the only one who returned. He poured himself a mug of rum and sat on the three-legged stool. Then he started to shake and sob uncontrollably.

Chapter 7

When the battle's done and won.

Tommy spent the following winter in the trenches and dugouts around Sevastopol. The freezing cold, the damp, the diseases, the filth and the ceaseless slaughter became part of his everyday life.
His lovely Kildangan with beloved parents and family in their cosy house on the lovely estate of Mr More O'Ferrall were constantly on his mind but only in the way that a pleasant dreams lingers: fading and unreal. Here was reality as his comrades were blown to bits by Russian shells or died of fever in their own dirt. Meanwhile the siege continued as attack after attack failed and the Russians in the city seemed to grow stronger and bolder every day. Their armies in the field seemed to be impossible to destroy. Defeat after defeat brought fresh reinforcements and new forces. It seemed as if the resources of the Tsar were inexhaustible. The Russians were defeated at the battles of the Little Inkerman, Inkerman and Tchernaya and after each battle they were able to re-build their shattered armies. Time and again, their defeated forces re-grouped, reinforced and still remained out there ready to pounce if the Allies weakened. Meanwhile, reinforcements for the Allies had to travel by sea from Britain, France or Italy. Even Turkish reinforcements had to travel the sea

route. The frost came and stayed as did the snow. The freezing winter was like nothing they had ever experienced. It was an awful country; blisteringly hot in summer and chillingly cold in winter. At night they drank as much as they could and talked and reminisced about home and family. Those who sank too deeply into their cups frequently cried for their loved ones or from homesickness. To pass the time, some of the men knitted as they had been taught in the barracks at Naas. It saved them from thinking too much about home and their present awful circumstances. It proved useful too as they improvised new garments to keep out the winter chill.

The wool was provided by the Quartermaster's Stores at a halfpenny an ounce to keep them occupied and out of trouble and especially away from the drink. They made woollen caps that came all the way over their faces to protect them from the frost and they called them Balaclavas after the battle. It was a bit of a joke at first but it soon caught on. Some men made short woollen coats which they wore under their red jackets to keep out the numbing cold. They called these cardigans after the gallant Lord who led the famous charge down the valley against the Russian guns. This engagement was now known to one and all as "The charge of the Light Brigade".

Fresh troops from Ireland and from all over the empire poured into the siege lines surrounding Sevastopol and the armies facing the Russians outside of the city. They were joined by thousands of gallant Frenchmen. They matched the Russian moves but never seemed to tip the balance in favour of the Allies. All that stuff about the

Russians being a backward country was now seen to be nonsense. In their army at least they had as many and as modern armaments as the Allies, or so it seemed to the men opposing them. A new country joined the Allies, it was called Sardinia and was a country in Italy. Neither Tommy nor the other Irishmen had ever heard of them or their country. The French were everywhere with their colourful uniforms, their fat cigars and their jugs of wine. Their officers were even more dandified than the officers in the British Army but all noticed that they treated their men better than the English did. They had scores of doctors. It was said that they had more troops in the Crimea than the British. Most of all they had so much food that they always seemed to be eating and very tasty looking and smelling it was too unlike their own rations.

Grub in the camp had now improved a little. Problems at the port of Balaclava had been somewhat sorted. The winter staple was a stew which warmed them up considerably during this harsh winter weather and was much looked forward to. There was even a smattering of potatoes in the stew and porter was now available to wash it down. The Irish were proud that the porter was brewed by Arthur Guinness in Dublin and they loved it. The stew contained a little meat and Jimmy Dunne said it was horsemeat from the slaughtered animals. Nobody really cared, it was still meat. Anyway it tasted alright and it was better than wasting the flesh of the poor beasts while the men were starving. The horses could be of use in death as in life. It was not as if they were used to eating much meat at home. All they were used to was a bit of boiled bacon from a pig they had slaughtered themselves and maybe a few rabbits in summer that were sold door to door by a man who poached them from the woods owned by Mr More O'Ferrall.

But miracle of miracles the winter stew contained spuds, this went down very well with the Irish lads. They had been deprived of these at home since the blight had wiped out all the potato crops in Ireland but now there seemed to be no shortage of potatoes here. However, no matter how much food they got, it never seemed to be enough, the men were always ravenously hungry in this freezing winter. The horrid biscuits and salted beef remained on the menu however. Nobody was going to get fat on this war in the Crimea.

All through this grim winter the main thing on Tommy Brennan's mind was not the food, not even his own safety and survival. Even when the slushy spring arrived it was the same, all he could think and worry about was the fate of his friend; Billy Britain. Would he survive and reappear at the campfire with his smile, his jokes and his dirty stories? Would he have a leg or an arm amputated, would he die of disease or dirt in the grim hospital, where everyone dreaded going? Getting sick or being wounded in the Crimea was merely a prelude to death and always accompanied by pain and suffering. Every soldier knew that. His thoughts on Billy extended far more than worry. Almost every night in his tent and beneath his blanket he thought of their warm embraces, the smoothness of Billy's skin and the passion and satisfaction he felt when he was inside him.

Billy had been removed on board the troopship "The Australia" to the military hospital near Constantinople. The place was called Scutari. The Irish lads had some laugh over that name, what a horrible word, just like "scuttery" which was what they called diarrhoea or "the scutters". It didn't seem like a sign of good luck to have a hospital with a name like that. Billy had written from there or at least got a nurse called Mrs Farrell to write for him. Maybe he couldn't write, thought Tommy, some of these fulltime soldiers weren't schooled at all. Fair play to Billy to have found a woman in the middle of all the carnage! The hospital was a dirty and overcrowded place and as its name suggested it stank to high heaven from the drains that ran underneath it and the sweaty, sick and dying men in its crowded wards. But they were well fed and kept as clean as possible. It had been recently taken over by an Englishwoman called Miss Florence Nightingale and she set great store on keeping the place and the men scrubbed and washed and that must be a good thing. Billy said that the nurses and doctors were terrified of her! The sick soldiers obeyed her as if she were their military superior which was the way she carried on.

In spite of all this, Tommy felt that Billy and by extension, all the other men, had a sneaking regard for Miss Nightingale. She was helping them, while their superiors had abandoned them in this rotten place instead of sending them back home.
There were Irish nuns too, from the Sisters of Charity and Miss Nightingale gave them a terrible time, treating them like skivvies and hunting them whenever they

started to pray with the wounded men. This didn't go down well with the Irish but Billy seemed to get a laugh out of it. He had never seen nuns and nurses fighting before, in fact he probably never saw nurses or nuns before, thought Tommy. He seemed to be enjoying himself in spite of his terrible wounds but perhaps that was just his way of carrying on. Everything was a laugh and a joke to Billy. It was a part of his sunny personality. Maybe he would pull through, but nobody in the Regiment had ever heard of a soldier who had gone to that place and returned. If the wounds didn't get them then gangrene and fever did. The swarming flies and rats as big as dogs were everywhere, fattening off the blood of the living and the flesh of the dead. Being sent to the hospital at Scutari was a death sentence and all the men knew it even if the higher-ups didn't care. If they did, they didn't do anything about it. For sure Miss Nightingale was operating without their blessing. She must be well connected back in England. Men were better off being treated here in the Crimee. There was a black woman called Mary Seacole who had set up what she called "a hotel", it was really a shebeen but it was also a nursing station as Mother Seacole looked after the men. They all swore by her. Of course they fancied her, sex and food were what they thought about most. The Irish had never seen a black woman before and some of them went up to her just to gawk. She had all sorts of cures, even for the fever. She was a warm-hearted woman who was like a mother or a big sister to the wounded men, forever dispensing drink and company to the homesick boys. She was fearless too; Billy was told that at the Battle of Inkerman which had happened in November that she ridden onto the battlefield while the fighting was still going on, to help the wounded. She wasn't a bit like that bossy old bitch Miss Nightingale treating the men as if they were stupid and dirty children and persecuting the holy nuns who had come all this way just to help the sick and dying and to give them the comfort of a few prayers on their deathbeds.

Mother Seacole, would often hug a frightened or wounded boy to calm him down and give him some peace and comfort. Miss Florence Nightingale was a dry old stick, he could just imagine the dirty remarks that Billy and the other men made about her behind her back. Tommy wondered if it was because she was English that she behaved like that. There was something wrong with them, particularly the higher-ups, Tommy was beginning to think. They weren't able to understand that a bit of kindness went a long way when dealing with people. He had seen the same attitude in the way the officers dealt with the men. He thought of the time that Jimmy Dunne was flogged. It had happened because that was the rule. The officers never thought beyond the rules or what effect their behaviour would have on the men.

But the English soldiers and the Irish were different. Many of the Irish could read and write, at least among those who had volunteered.

It was different for the English boys, most of them didn't seem to have any learning at all. It wasn't like the old days when only the gentry had any schooling. Maybe that was the reason, Tommy thought, the

English gentry seemed to think they were way better than the ordinary men, a different breed entirely. He had noticed too that the English soldiers treated their officers with more respect than the Irish did. It was like the way the old people treated the gentry back in Ireland, touching their forelock when they passed and thinking the sun shone out of their arses. Well, that day was gone for the Irish and no harm either.

The winter of 1854/55 outside Sevastopol was the worst form of life. The nights and the days were freezing in a way it never froze at home. Sentries and horses were regularly found stiff and frozen to death in the early morning. The biting cold chilled all exposed body parts sometimes causing frostbite. This was a serious thing, the effected part was dead: a hand or a foot suffering from it had to be amputated. Then of course, the man would be no use for soldiering and the unfortunate lad would be sent home to a life of beggary as they could hardly work at anything else with a limb missing. Like everything else in this bloody war, the fighting was the least bad part, but that was grim too. Thousands of tons of shot and shell were poured into the city and again and again the forts surrounding it were bombarded heavily and on a regular basis.
Yet the massive Redan and Malakov Forts held out and these must be taken before an army could advance into the city, as they blocked the way.
It seemed that no punishment they could inflict on the Russians would dislodge them or break their spirits.
The Irish lads muddled through though, sustained by thoughts of their own warm and pleasant country, a few

prayers to see them through and lots of rum or porter to warm their bellies in the evening and give them courage for the next assault. Jimmy Dunne said that there was no such thing as a brave man, only a drunken one and there was a lot in what he said. Copious draughts of rum, passed from man to man before the charge, fuelled every attack. Tommy reckoned that it was the same on the Russian side. Only drink could make a sane man charge again and again against unyielding stone forts that the mightiest guns in the British army couldn't demolish. Some of the men seemed to be drunk or nearly drunk all during the day. And yet there were some acts of kindness. Billy wrote from Scutari that Lord Cardigan had visited him in hospital there. That was kind of the old gent. He had told Billy that he could keep his bugle, the one that had sounded the charge of the Light Brigade. It was a great honour. Tommy and all the lads agreed. Surely Billy would pull through now and be back with them telling stories of stories of his time in hospital and boasting about the nurses there who had fallen for him.

Lord Lucan had been sent home in disgrace for failing to follow up Lord Cardigan's attack at the Battle of Balaclava. "I wish I could be sent home out of this hellhole too as punishment like that stupid, cowardly bastard, I got twenty lashes for my trouble and he gets sent home" Jimmy Dunne had remarked with a wan but bitter smile on his face, but even he knew that punishment for a nobleman and a soldier were different things indeed.
Then of course there was the famous poem "The

Charge of the Light Brigade" written by Lord Tennyson and circulated free to the soldiers at Christmas 1854. Soon it was learned and recited by heart by many of the men. Even those in the Irish Regiments felt pride when listening or reciting the poem though most of them had been besieging Sevastopol and so not directly involved in the battle, but there were scores of Irishmen in the battle , like Billy Britain in the Light Brigade though it was not an Irish company.

Tommy learned the poem by heart and would often recite it to his comrades during those long winter months. His favourite verses were the final two:

>Cannon to right of them,
>Cannon to left of them,
>Cannon behind them
>Volley'd and thunder'd ;
>Storm'd at with shot and shell,
>While horse and hero fell,
>They that had fought so well

>Came thro' the jaws of Death,
>Back from the mouth of Hell,
>All that was left of them,
>Left of six hundred.
>When can their glory fade?
>0h the wild charge they made!
>All the world wonder'd.
>Honour the charge they made!
>Honour the Light Brigade,
>Noble six hundred!

It never failed to bring a tear to his eye as he thought of his own hero in the heat of the action. If he was to take nothing else home to Kildangan, at least he would have this. He could imagine himself reciting the poem to great applause at his father's fireside. Even here in the Crimee, tough soldiers cried when they heard the recitation and the men felt they were appreciated back home for their fighting and the sacrifices they were making.

Billy lingered on in agony until February, never failing to send his weekly good-humoured letters to Tommy who lived to receive them and read them aloud to the Kildangan boys. Then the letters stopped. All knew what this meant but Tommy still held onto the small hope that Billy had been let out and would one evening appear at their camp full of funny stories, laughter and rum.

Towards the end of the month Mrs Farrell wrote to him to tell him that their good friend Corporal Britain had died of an infection in the chest caused by a wound inflicted during the Battle of Balaclava and asking for Tommy's prayers for their friend. He was laughing and joking with the other soldiers and nurses right till the end, Mrs Farrell told him. She seemed a kind person thought Tommy, thanking God that Billy had someone like that beside him when he passed away. He didn't mention Billy's death to any of the lads and only told Jimmy Dunne when he asked him directly. He didn't want to talk about it ever again. Billy had been the best friend in his life, talking about it wouldn't bring him back, better to just think and pray for the brave, big

Dundalk man. All the other soldiers in the company knew about Billy's passing but never ever brought up the subject in Tommy's company. Now there was only one priority; to get out of this place alive and back to Ireland, to his family and his beloved Kildangan.

All through that winter of 1854/55 bombardment followed bombardment and still the Russian forts surrounding the city held out. Meanwhile the Russian armies in the north were held off in engagement after engagement. It wasn't till June that a breakthrough occurred when the French took the Mamelon battery and the British advanced to take the quarries outside the city. On 28th June 1855 old Lord Raglan died and the searing sun shone on the total indifference of the men to his passing. They were too concerned about their own miserable conditions. At least a new commander might bring some fresh ideas to the campaign but the appointment of Sir James Simpson brought only more of the same; bombardment, attack and failure to force a Russian surrender, then back to the trenches to repeat the whole process again.

September brought the prospect of another bloody, freezing and pointless winter in the Crimea. The men had had enough and so had the officers. It looked as if the Russians could never be defeated in their own territory. Then just as morale was at rock bottom a breakthrough came. On the 8th September after the sixth bombardment of the city, the French finally captured the Malakov Fort though the British failed again to capture the Redan. The next day the Russians abandoned the southside of the city and the Allies

marched in.
From here on the fighting was patchy and half-hearted. All knew, including the Russians, that the war was over. Their Tsar had died earlier on during the year and talk around the army was that the new one, Alexander II hadn't the stomach for fight that his father had and anyway their losses were appalling too.

As winter took grip again with all the misery it promised, the men settled in for a second time. Things were better than in the previous winter; supplies were more plentiful, they had learned a lot about how to survive the freezing temperatures or maybe their bodies were more used to it and there was little or no fighting. Still the boredom was a real killer, driving many of the men to the drink which was in even more plentiful supply. It was strange, Tommy remarked to Jimmy Dunne, who had now taken Billy Britain's place as his friend, that there was so little fighting in a war. It was mainly waiting around for a battle or an attack to start. Christmas was memorable that year. Tommy had a letter from home. His father wrote it with the help of the schoolmaster, Mr Merriman and Tommy read it with pride to the Kildangan boys. They had assembled after Mass, all having managed to avoid picket duty that day. Mr More O'Ferrall had sent half dozen porter cakes and four gallon flasks of whiskey to them, half way round the world for Christmas Day. All the boys from Kildangan were invited to partake in his hospitality.
The officers obliged by supplying a tent for the festivities; Mr More O'Ferrall having taken the wise

precaution of writing to their commanding officer on behalf of the twenty-two men from Kildangan and the neighbouring estates. Sitting round on benches in the white army tent they felt a comradeship and bond that had rarely been part of their war. There were toasts to one another, to Kildangan and to Mr More O'Ferrall for his generosity and thoughtfulness, to Ireland and to fallen comrades and especially to going home. As the day wore on and the warmth of the whiskey, now supplemented by rum and porter from the Quartermaster took effect, the singing started.
Jimmy Dunne had a whole store of the lovely songs from Mr Thomas Moore and sang them out with gusto. He raised the roof with "The Minstrel Boy" which seemed very apt to the company:

> The Minstrel Boy to the war has gone
> In the ranks of death you will find him,
> His father sword he has gird it on
> With his wild harp slung behind him

Soon they were all merry on what seemed the best whiskey and rum they had ever tasted. Later on Jimmy sang "The Harp that once through Tara's halls" and he even tried "The Lark in the clear air" but couldn't quite hit the high notes, but it didn't matter anyway, everyone was happy and joined in when they could. Jimmy Kennedy, whose father kept the Public House in the village had brought a melodeon with him all the way from Kildare and was soon battering out jigs and polkas. The merry company soon had dancers on the floor while the rest kept time with clapping. The whiskey lasted till about four o'clock in the afternoon and then everyone stumbled back to their billets to sleep it off. Those with a few pennies in their pockets headed off to Mother Seacole's shebeen in search of further refreshment.

On 29th February 1856 they received news of the Armistice. A peace treaty had been signed in Paris between Russia and the Allies. The war was over! What excitement and cheering in the ranks this caused when the officer read the news out at parade! Two days later they marched into what was left of Sevastopol and the Russians marched out. Now they saw at first-hand what devastation had been caused. There was hardly a wall standing not to talk of a house. What brave boys these Rooskies were to hold on for so long in a city now composed only of rubble and the shattered remains of their once fine port!
Almost immediately the sappers in the Royal Engineers started to demolish the quays in the harbour. Using thousands of tons of gunpowder, the explosions were deadly and deafening, almost worse than they had experienced during the many bombardments.
After a week the docks were blown to bits.
Not a stone or a brick bigger than a fist was to be seen anywhere as the remains of the harbour walls crashed into the water. How stupid, Tommy thought, the Russians would re-build them as soon as the Allies left. The hundreds of Russian guns in the fortress city were carted and manhandled back to Balaclava to be put on ships bound for home as trophies of the war. Then it was all over, and there was a strange feeling among the

men that it was ending too quickly though they had been longing for this day almost since they had set foot in the Crimea. It was an anti-climax. The 18th Royal Irish Regiment of Foot embarked at the port of Balaclava on the 19th June 1856, two long years after they had arrived. In the midst of all the cheering, happy faces on board the HMS Scotia that day Tommy stood alone among the crowd sobbing silently.

He stared at the crowded harbour as it receded into the distance, thinking of his friend Billy Britain resting forever in the sun-scorched graveyard at Scutari. Life was not a nice thing at all, he knew he should be happy like the other boys but he felt only loneliness and disappointment.

Epilogue.

The Crimean War Banquet.

22 October 1856.

Once again the bands played and the people of Dublin were out in their thousands to cheer on the soldiers as they marched along the Quays. Tommy and his friend Jimmy Dunne marched shoulder to shoulder from Kingsbridge Train Station towards the Port of Dublin. There, the grateful and proud citizens of Dublin had laid out a feast for their Irish Crimean War veterans. It was to be the greatest dinner that Ireland had ever seen with 5,000 guests attending in the giant bonding warehouse called Stack A in the Custom House Docks. It was the only building in Ireland capable of holding such a vast number.

Everyone in Dublin must have been on the Quays that morning to watch the procession of scarlet coated soldiers, each wearing his Crimean War medal, marching down behind their regimental bands. Every window, even some rooftops held a cheering waving crowd and the pavements were jammed full behind a police cordon. "What a great day to be alive" smiled Tommy cheerfully at his friend. "I'd rather be in Kildangan hunting More O'Ferrall's rabbits" replied Jimmy, "No you bloody well wouldn't, don't be such a grouch" said Tommy.

"This is a day to remember for all our lives, lots of

fellows would give their right arm to be here." "A lot of fellows did" said Jimmy. Tommy was right though, because so many Crimean War veterans were stationed in Ireland at the time only about one third could be accommodated.

He was delighted to have been chosen and everyone was a bit surprised when Jimmy was picked too considering his bit of bother, as he called the flogging he received outside Sevastopol. They supposed that Mr More O'Ferrall has put in a word for them.
It had been a hard, boring few months since they had returned to Ireland. Still cooped up in the barracks at Naas awaiting discharge from the army, now at last they had been promised they would be let go on the 1st of November. Afterall they had only joined up for the War in the Crimea and to be stuck in the army months after the war had ended was ruining it all for them. At least they would be out by Christmas.
That was something, though they had missed the harvest and all the fun surrounding it. There was a great atmosphere as they marched down the Quays that bright October morning. The crowd greeted them rapturously, the men waving and cheering, the women waving their handkerchiefs and blowing kisses. How Billy would have loved it, Tommy thought to himself.

Those who had received Legion of Honour medals from the French Emperor were pointed out and cheered especially.
Many of the young men, with arms missing and their sleeves neatly folded and pinned on their uniforms were

pointed out and the crowd "oohed" and "aahed" at them in pity or in horror. The veterans who had lost legs were taken to the feast in carriages.

Chatting along merrily while they marched, the host of soldiers reached the warehouse near the end of the Quays in about an hour, where the banquet was to take place.

They assembled in the yard in front of the giant warehouse and given directions on how to find their tables when they entered the great building which was a wonder in itself. A member of the Organising Committee sat at each table. At Tommy's table was Isaac Butt MP for Youghal and a famous barrister. He was a great Irish patriot, Tommy's father had told him in his recent letter and he had defended the rebel leader William Smith O'Brien after the rebellion of the Young Irelanders in 1848. His father got his information from the schoolmaster Mr Merriman who was a rebel himself.

He subscribed to The Nation newspaper and regularly read it aloud to all the locals who were interested. He was a Young Irelander and a rebel, especially after a few drops of whiskey of which he was rather too fond. They wanted to get the English out of Ireland and Jimmy Dunne was in total agreement with that.

"There'll never be peace in Ireland until we get rid of them and run the country ourselves." "But Jimmy, there is peace in Ireland, there is in Kildare anyway, and who would run the country, there aren't enough Catholic gentry like Mr More O'Ferrall and Daniel O'Connell is dead these eight years past?" "You don't have to be Catholic to be a patriot" Jimmy replied "Look at Mr

Butt, he's a Protestant from Donegal and a great Irishman." There was no use arguing with Jimmy he always had the last word and anyway he might be right. Tommy wasn't too bothered, one way or another, anyway as the food was arriving soon, that was more important than politics.

It was about 12.30 before they entered the Banquet Hall and what a gorgeous sight it presented! The tables were covered in white linen tablecloths and an array of cutlery, crockery and glassware. The pillars supporting the roof of the vast hall were painted in bright colours: red, blue and yellow and the walls were white.
Above the top table were arches made of laurels with the names of Queen Victoria and her husband Prince Albert and those of the French Emperor Louis Napoleon and his wife, the Empress Eugenie. From the pillars hung the flags of the Allies; Great Britain, France, Turkey and Sardinia.
A special gallery had been constructed at the end of the hall where members of the public who bought tickets were accommodated. These cost the princely sum of 10 shillings per gentleman and 5 shillings for the ladies. The pennants from the different regiments hung round the walls and the names of the victorious generals were written all along the borders; Lord Raglan's being given prominence. As the soldiers representing the different regiments took their places the chatter in the giant hall reach enormous levels.
Then as new groups were marched in loud cheers and clapping broke out. A special roar was given to the 20 pensioners from the Royal Hospital in Kilmainham.

These men had fought not only in the recent wars against the Sikhs in India but against Napoleon in the Peninsular Wars and at Waterloo, almost 50 years previously. John Lyons, only across the border in county Carlow was there too, he had won the Victoria Cross and the French Legion of Honour, he was the bravest of them all. He had thrown a Russian shell out of his trench and saved the lives many of his fellow soldiers. It had exploded seconds later with devastating effect but his comrades had been saved.

At 1.00 p.m. all were seated and ready but couldn't start till the Lord Lieutenant, Lord Carlisle arrived. Nobody minded as they knew it was only courtesy on his behalf, he wanted to make sure everyone was there before his arrival as nobody would be allowed in after he was seated. The bands of the 2nd and 3rd Dragoons Guards and the Rifle Brigade played away above the din making a jolly mix of music and chatter. At 1.15 exactly they struck up the Viceregal Salute and all stood as Lord Carlisle entered the hall and took his seat at the top table.

Immediately the waiters rushed out with huge steaming trays carrying the food. The drink had lain untouched on the tables till now and that was hard on the men who were gasping for some sustenance. Each was given two pints of porter; "Not enough to wet your whistle" complained Jimmy. They were also given a pint of port or sherry which they all agreed wasn't real drink at all. "They must be afraid that if you get too much drink in you that you'll drop your trousers like you did that night outside Sevastopol and show your arse to the Lord

Lieutenant" whispered Tommy with a smile on his face. "Maybe he'd like it" replied Jimmy, quick as a flash, "You know what these English lords are like." "No I don't" replied Tommy", "They all piss sitting down" said Jimmy. Tommy didn't reply but thought, not for the first time that sometimes his friend, Jimmy Dunne was as thick as two short planks.

The preparation of the food had been contracted out to the city's hotels and most of it transported hot to the hall. Three tons of potatoes came from the Royal Arcade Hotel in College Green and brought up in four vans surrounded by running street urchins who accompanied them all the way.
The steam coming from the vans added to the spectacle, it looked like the vans were on fire and they were cheered by the onlookers as they headed down the Quays. Potatoes were again grown in Ireland, thanks to new blight resistant breeds that had been introduced. The old Lumper potato which was so susceptible to the blight was now a thing of the past. 250 hams, 230 legs of mutton, 500 meat pies, 100 venison pasties, 200 turkeys, 200 geese, 250 joints of beef, 100 capons and 2,000 loaves were provided. For dessert there were 260 plum puddings and 100 rice puddings. It was a feast for heroes and Tommy and his mates revelled in it.
The bands played all through the dinner and some of the soldiers joined in to tunes they knew like "St Patrick's Day" and "Savourneen Deelish", others chattered away to their table companions. Tommy and Jimmy bantered away and tried to identify those at the top table with little success. They swapped stories of

the war with their table companions but they stopped
short of relating the story about Jimmy's flogging
though Tommy was sure they all knew of it, it was one
of the famous stories of the war. All were delighted at
the downfall of the cowardly and cruel Lord Lucan who
had returned to England in disgrace soon after he had
let down his comrades at the Battle of Balaclava.

All agreed that there would never be a war again like
that in the Crimea: no Tsar of Russia would ever again
take on the might of the Allies.
France and Great Britain were now friends after
hundreds of years fighting one another. "Maybe we will
be the last soldiers ever to have fought in a big war in
Europe though I suppose there will always be little
wars" speculated Tommy. "Maybe we'll have a war in
Ireland someday against the English" chipped in Jimmy.
"Naw" said Tommy. "That day has gone, people are too
busy making a good living for themselves and their
families, anyway how could the Irish fight against the
might of the English, you saw the size of the army in
the Crimee,"

Those around nodded their heads in agreement. After
the dinner and desserts came the Lord Lieutenant's
speech. In his upper-class English accent he praised all
present and their absent comrades for their bravery. He
was cheered loudly. "Not a bad old fellow for an
Englishman" conceded Jimmy. Then came the toasts to
which the men were expected to raise their sherry or
port glasses but some of the privates, unused to having
full cups of drink in front of them, had guzzled them

down as soon as they were poured. Queen Victoria, the Lord Lieutenant and the French Emperor were all toasted. They were very proud at Tommy's table when Mr. Isaac Butt stood to toast "The heroes of the Crimea". There was also a toast to Miss Florence Nightingale and the Sisters of Charity. "They should have included Mother Seacole in that one" said Tommy but they drank up nevertheless.

It was all over at 4.15pm and the merry band of soldiers, their bellies full and their spirits high, filed out in proper order with their regiments and assembled in the yard outside the banquet hall. Then they marched back down the Quays to Kingsbridge Station. The crowds en route seemed even thicker than on the way there, all hurrahing and waving good-naturedly, though it was getting dusky now. The cheering and clapping continued all the way down the Quays till they reached their destination. Crowds of happy, tipsy soldiers waited for their trains to take them back to barracks all over the country to wait for their next war.
For Tommy and Jimmy it was a return to Naas only to await their discharge from the army and return to their beautiful village of Kildangan and the green fields round it.

For Tommy it couldn't come too quickly, he was homesick and sentimental for Kildangan. Even before his return home, his proud father had been regaling his friends and neighbours about his son's exploits. So much so that he was nicknamed "Crimee Tommy". It was a name that his son answered to with pride though it had been coined by the locals mainly in exasperation at his father's excessive boasting.

Chapter 8

The day has come. Tuesday 5th March 1867

It was Shrove Tuesday and all over Kildangan and indeed all over the country the women were cooking and preparing food in a frenzy. It was if their lives depended on it. Tomorrow was Ash Wednesday and the start of Lent and for seven long weeks there would be fasting in preparation for Easter. Just one full meal was allowed each day and two small ones called "collations" and no meat at all could be consumed during the holy season.
Today Catherine Brennan and her daughter-in-law Julia were gathering all the excess eggs and milk that must be used up; some of the eggs were painted in waterglass and immersed in the solution in earthenware crocks, this would preserve them for future use. These, and any other eggs collected during the seven weeks of fasting, would be used after Lent or on Easter Sunday when they would be hard-boiled and given to the children to be painted in garish colours. Any food that wasn't preserved or used up today would be fed to the pigs and no self-respecting housewife could allow that to happen.

"Waste not, want not" was what Catherine constantly reminded Julia, preparing her for her life, when she too would run her own household and become a thrifty housewife like her mother-in-law. So today and tonight

everything in the line of a perishable food must be used up or preserved till Lent was over. Besides the dairy products, the only meat in the house was the remains of a slaughtered pig which was salted and would hang untouched from the rafters till Easter Sunday when a great feast of bacon and cabbage would celebrate the end of the seven week fast.
Indeed some would be used on that morning, fried on the pan with lashings of eggs in the bacon grease, but that was pale in comparison to the Easter Sunday morning breakfast. Even now, seven weeks before the event, Catherine could smell that feast and hear the rashers sizzling on Easter Sunday morning.

Tonight would be a great time of gorging and stuffing before the dreary hunger and fasting of the holy season of Lent. The two women had already made three bowls of pancake batter from the creamy milk and every egg they could spare. That night lashings of butter would be put on the hot pan which would then be covered with the batter, turned over when golden-brown, the enormous pancakes would stuff even the most ravenous of the men. Everyone was like a child this night greedily stuffing their faces till they were hardly able to get up out of their chairs and felt ready to burst. There would be sugar to put on the pancakes for those who could afford it. All over Ireland the men and the children were eagerly anticipating the feast that awaited them. Meanwhile the women worked together, chatting away and rubbing their fingers around the mixing bowl and tasting the delicious pancake batter or licking the mixing spoon, pretending that this was a necessity for tasting the flavour of the concoction. Standing in her own kitchen in Kildangan, Catherine Brennan was the mistress of all she surveyed. Fussing over the preparations for Lent and bossing her daughter-in-law Julia around, she was the picture of busy contentment. Her grey hair was in a neat bun on the back of her head and her flowery pinafore was wrapped tightly around her ample figure.

But there was something on her mind today other than the job in hand. Her brow was wrinkled and her eyes bullet sharp. Julia knew there was an outburst coming. "And where the hell is Tommy gone, this day of all days?" asked Catherine. "I told you, he didn't say a word, just sneaked out before daybreak, didn't as much as take his leave of me. Says I, you're not going up to the yard at this hour?" "I am not" was all he replied" answered Tommy's wife Julia, averting her mother-in-law's eyes. Catherine left down her wooden mixing spoon and looked sharply at Julia. "It's a quare way to behave if you ask me," she said. "Are you sure there's nothing going on between the two of you?" Julia kept her eyes lowered and said "As sure as God is my judge, Catherine Brennan, I don't know where he went." The two women started to work again in silence. " I thought I heard a horse outside in the small hours" said Catherine keeping her eyes steadily on her daughter-in-law, hoping to catch some glint of guilt in her. "Sure there's many a horse passes by in the night, I didn't hear no horse

James Stephens, the Fenian leader was called "The Head Centre"

Maybe his father knows where he went?" ventured Julia. "Divil a know he knows"answered Catherine. "Its no way to treat his wife or mother, heading off without bye or leave like a tinker after his dinner. Sometimes I think he hasn't been right since the Crimee all those years back. He hasn't a rake of common-sense and hanging round with that waster of a blacksmith's son, Jimmy Dunne. Sometimes I don't know whether he's coming or going, God help us I don't think he knows himself".

"Maybe he's gone off somewhere with him" said Julia. "With who?" asked Catherine. "With Jimmy Dunne the blacksmith's son, they could have gone someplace together" suggested Julia.

"God help us if they are" replied his mother "The two of them would be up to no good."

"I don't know about that Catherine, Tommy knows his own mind and he won't get into any harm."

"He's easily led by that Dunne fella, neither him nor his father are any good, always agitating and causing trouble. What's going to happen up in the yard anyway, what's his father going to say about him not showing up like that? Fitzgerald could easily put him out on the road. He's a bad egg and would only love to see Tommy in trouble, he has it in for the Brennans for many a year"

"No, he won't fire him, Catherine, my Tommy is a good worker and has a great way with the horses and Fitzgerald knows that. As for him being led astray by Jimmy Dunne, Tommy may be quiet and keep his opinions to himself but that doesn't mean he has no opinions. Tommy thinks about things and he thinks hard and long about them. It's just that he keeps himself to himself and doesn't go mouthing to everyone he meets like some people, like Jimmy Dunne. Tommy is quiet but he is very thoughtful and when he makes up is mind on something he follows it through and his family always comes first to him. As for his work in the Yard, sure his father will cover for him and say he's sick, there's many sick at this time of the year."

At this hour, about eleven o'clock in the morning on this cold spring's day, Tommy and Jimmy were on the outskirts of Kilcullen, a small town in south Kildare. They were both mounted on Jimmy's grey mare and in great spirits. Jimmy was in front and Tommy sitting behind. They were taking it nice and easy, the horse moving at a canter. They had plenty of time to make it to their rendezvous at Tallaght Hill in Dublin county and anyway they did not want to wear out the old nag. "Its just like the old days" Tommy said in Jimmy's ear "heading off for the Crimee and not a care in the world." "Indeed it is not, this is serious business and not fighting for a foreign queen in a faraway place, but out for our own country to be free."

"Do you think we'll win?" asked Tommy. "We've a better chance now than ever, there are ten thousand Fenians going to be under arms tonight and we could take the whole country by daybreak, think of that, Ireland free at one stroke."
"Sounds a bit too good to be true, if you ask me, it couldn't be that easy" answered Tommy. It was gently

snowing now and it was settling, it would slow down their pace.

"There's years work gone into it, there are Fenian cells in every village in Ireland and scores in every city too. There's thousands of guns and the men to lead us are here from America, they are all Irishmen who were officers in their Civil War" explained Jimmy. "There's not too many supporters in Kildangan, if the two of us are all we have to show for it." "Kildangan is a sleepy place where nothing happens. Everyone is too comfortable there for their own good but that will change too when the revolution comes. The More O'Ferralls won't be lording it over us like little gods, we'll be heroes when we get home; officers in the army of the Irish Republic."

"That would be one for the books" said Tommy but thinking that he really wouldn't like much to change in Kildangan, things were all right there in spite of what Jimmy was saying. All the same, he would love Ireland to be free from the English and see Irishmen running their own country like every other self-respecting place in the world. But it was no use arguing with Jimmy, he had answers to every question and he felt comfortable with that.

The horse moved on at its slow pace and the two men were silent for awhile. Then without saying why, Jimmy reined her into the side of the road.

"Time for a break" he said and they both dismounted. Tommy sat on the grass bank and took some bread from the pocket of his greatcoat. It was still snowing lightly but it didn't matter to him, he was hungry.

Jimmy tied the horse to a furze bush and came over to Tommy. "Put that away for a minute" he said in an officious tone.
"Jesus, Jimmy, you sound like my sergeant in the Crimee." "There's important business to be done before we go any farther". Tommy looked up at him quizzically but stuffed the bread back in his pocket. "You have to officially join the movement before we go any farther."
"Amn't I here with you this cold spring's morning on the way to a rising, isn't that enough?" "Its not and you know it's not, time for you Tommy boy to join the army of the Irish Republic." "The priests are against taking an oath and especially the Fenian one, they say it's a sin and you know that too and I don't like it myself anyway, not on this day before Lent or any other day." "Stop your excuses Tommy Brennan, the priests will come round when we win, sure they're not going to side against their own people when the war starts, anyone who is serious about this takes the oath."
Tommy stared at his friend and decided to give in to Jimmy Dunne as he always did, "Sure I suppose I'm halfway on the road to sedition as it is, I might as well be hung for a sheep as a lamb, go on, get on with it." He got to his feet and stood facing Jimmy.

So it happened, on the road to Kilcullen that Tommy swore the Fenian oath in front of his friend Jimmy Dunne. "I, Thomas Brennan of Kildangan in the county of Kildare, in the presence of the Almighty God, do solemnly swear allegiance to the Irish Republic, now virtually established, and that I will do my utmost at

every risk, while life lasts, to defend its independence
and integrity; and, finally, that I will yield implicit
obedience in all things, not contrary to the laws of God,
to the commands of my superior officers. So help me
God. Amen."
When it was over Tommy sat dawn again, he was now
in it up to his neck, in spite of all his father had told
him and his own reservations. Ah well, he was a man
himself and could make his own decisions. He felt a bit
better now that it was finally done and he was officially
part of the movement.

"There is no going back now" said Jimmy. Tommy
knew what he meant, he was now a rebel against the
law of the land. His eyes glazed over as he felt for the
first time that he was doing something dangerous, it had
been an adventure and a lot of old talk up till now.
There could be jail at the end of this or hanging even.
The Constabulary and the government were hardly
going to let an army of Fenians take over the country
without a fight.
If someone got killed as was bound to happen, there
would be hell to pay. Not that he minded shooting
people, he had done plenty of that in the Crimea,
though it might be different if he was killing Irishmen.
It couldn't be avoided though. You don't go round
shooting off guns without people getting hurt.
He reached into his pocket and took out the bread that
Julia had placed there in the small hours of the morning
as she tiptoed around the house for fear of waking the
old couple or the children.

Jimmy sat down beside him, watching him and as he returned the look a warm feeling came over him as he realised that they were now comrades-in-arms again just as they had been many years previously in the faraway Crimea.

At Kilcullen the horsemen crossed the River Liffey and headed out the Ballymore Eustace road. The countryside was quiet and if anyone thought it strange to see two men riding the single horse then nobody challenged them in the sleepy villages they passed through, in fact everyone saluted them as they passed with a "Good Morrow" or "Fine day" even though it wasn't a fine day at all.

It was very strange thought Tommy, here they were going to change the world or at least the Irish world and everywhere it seemed as if they were just heading off to a fair. At Kilcullen they even passed the constabulary barracks and saluted the single constable standing in the doorway, smoking his pipe. After Ballymore Eustace they crossed the border into County Wicklow and entered the hilly country.

"We're making good time" announced Jimmy, "We'll be able to stop off at an eating house in Blessington for some nourishment to set us up for the night ahead, I'll let you in on the full plan when we reach there" he said sounding very important indeed.

Already Tommy was beginning to have his doubts. Leaving home so early without taking leave of his parents was a bit ungrateful and undutiful even if he was going on an adventure. He also missed his dinner which he knew would be well over by now. The few

slices of bread was nothing in comparison to a big hearty plateful of bacon and spuds with lashings of butter, or maybe the delicious rabbit stew that his mother might make for this special day Shrove Tuesday and maybe even tea and porter cake afterwards instead of riding around the foothills in the snow with an empty belly.
"Finish the cake" his mother would say, "It will be of no use tomorrow, you don't want it to go to the pigs, do you?" It didn't bear thinking about.

He could imagine them at dinnertime, talking about him and his sudden disappearance. His father with his head down, suspecting what was afoot but keeping his silence lest he alarm his wife and Julia saying a silent prayer and pretending she knew nothing and the children asking where their Daddy was.
He felt more than a bit guilty about sneaking away but Jimmy said that there was no other way. The rising had to be kept secret and he was right about that; the country was full of police informers. But it was rough on Julia who hadn't tried to stand in his way. She understood things without him saying them, it seemed as if she knew what he was thinking, that was why he felt so close to her always. He was sure she was with child again though she hadn't said anything to him. His father had made a great match for him with Julia, a neat little dowry, all of twenty guineas, not like in the old days when people married just because they liked the look of one another like his own father and mother. It was hard on them, his sneaking off like that but if things worked out on the night and the war started well,

then they would understand and forgive him.

But he was very perplexed about their lack of weapons. Riding off to war without a pistol between the two of them seemed a bit stupid. Jimmy had assured him that there would be more than enough at Tallaght Hill where the revolution was to start. They were both trained soldiers but what about the other Fenians from all over Ireland, surely they wouldn't be expected to be tradesmen one day and soldiers the next? How could they form an army they would beat all the experienced soldiers the British could throw at them. Maybe Jimmy would explain it to him when they reached Blessington.

He hoped they had modern weapons and in plentiful supply at Tallaght Hill and not some old hunting pieces which were two a penny in Ireland and some of them forty or fifty years old. Officers too, they would get nowhere without officers and fully trained ones as well, not like Jimmy thought he was in his fanciful moments, he was just a foot soldier like himself. It was a different thing entirely giving orders to a regiment of men and knowing what they were to do and more importantly to be obeyed. Would anyone obey Jimmy Dunne, especially a crowd of Dublin Jackeens who looked down their noses at men from the country?He couldn't see it. He would speak his mind to Jimmy in the eating-house at Blessington. It was getting dark when they rode into the village. It must have been around five o'clock. Blessington was a quiet sort of place with neat shop fronts and a wide main street. It was empty of people on this cold spring's evening. The old horse was wearying now: just dragging her feet. The two riders were in need of rest as well and sustenance too. It had been a long day since Jimmy had tapped on his window in the early hours, and because he had been expecting it he hadn't slept soundly that night.

They dismounted and tied the old nag to an iron rail which was built into the front of the shop window. Jimmy fixed a nosebag to the horse, the nag would have something to eat too. They were glad to get in out of the snow which had been ceaseless for a few hours now.

The place was called "The Slaney Arms" after the river that flowed through the town and proudly boasted to be "purveyors of teas, wines and spirits". It was a modern place with a shop on one side of the premises and a public house on the other side, the entrance doorway in between. Two customers sat in silence at the bar and paid no attention to the strangers. Tommy and Jimmy seated themselves away from the bar, beside an empty fireplace where they could talk without being overheard. It was dim inside with no light yet against the darkening evening but it was a welcome break from the hours they had spent on horseback. A serving girl came over and chatted to them. "We're travelling all the way from Monastrevin to Dublin" Jimmy explained. "Then you'll be looking for a place to spend the night" she volunteered. "No" said Jimmy, "We're going to press on and travel through the night, we'll make Dublin by daybreak." The serving girl was clearly unimpressed by such foolishness on a cold, snowy and darkening day. "We're looking for a bite to eat, to warm

us up for the night. She looked at them suspiciously and said, "Do you want pints and I'll see what we have in the kitchen?"
"Good girl" said Jimmy "That would be grand". Awhile later she returned with a pair of pints of porter and soon after she brought some coals around which she built a fire in the grate. Meanwhile the two men had entered into their long awaited conversation.

"The day has come" Jimmy announced in a grave low voice "We've been waiting for this moment for years and now it's here" Jimmy explained to his friend. "Up to five thousand men from Dublin City and county will assemble on Tallaght Hill tonight. We will take the countryside by storm and tomorrow morning we'll march into Dublin. The British won't know what hit them. That's why the countryside we rode through was so quiet, this time our plans have been kept secret. By mid-day tomorrow we will be in Dublin Castle and the Irish Republic will be proclaimed and the Fenian Executive will take over the running of the country straight away".
"Five thousand men" Tommy could not fail to be impressed. "And that's only the beginning of it. There will be risings all over the country. The movement is strong in every county. It's the best chance we ever had of being free. Tomorrow will be the first day in the life of the Irish Republic and me and you Tommy Brennan will not only be there to see it but you will be part of it." "Will there be enough arms and munitions at Tallaght for the five thousand, that's a mighty number to supply?" asked Tommy. "That's very important and

will there be captains for the men? Its alright for us, we're experienced soldiers, but most of the fellas from Dublin wouldn't know one end of a gun from the other, or how to march or follow orders." "You'd be surprised Tommy my boy. They have been training since the Fenians were started in 1858, I trained some of them myself when I spent those years in Dublin. The officers have all come from America and are all Yankees from the Civil War, that was the winning side by the way. They are masters of mobility and surprise. That's how they beat the Confederates in the Civil War over there. To a man they are all Irish, just think of it, an Irish army led by American captains. We'll sweep all before us and drive the British into the sea and back to their own country."

His excitement and confidence was infectious. Tommy felt it and shared it, imagine beating the mighty British Army and an Irish Republic run by Irishmen, that would be great!

He sat back, reassured and thrilled by what he had just heard. So Ireland might be free at last, what an exciting idea, an Irish army led by Americans. His brother Nick was over there but wasn't involved in anything like this. At least not as he mentioned in his letters home. This thing better go right, he thought but didn't say. If it didn't it could mean years in jail or maybe worse. But it was worth the risk, all life was a gamble anyway and a matter of luck, either of them could have been killed in the Crimea. Now maybe something greater might happen to them. They would take part in the establishment of the Irish Republic.

About a quarter of an hour after they came in, the girl brought them two plates piled high with bacon, potatoes and cabbage. It was warmed-up food, not that it mattered, they were so hungry. They washed the food down with a mug of buttermilk each having finished the porter "Thank God its today we're here, tomorrow is Ash Wednesday" said Tommy, "and we'd get no meat here or anywhere, we'd be lucky to get the spuds on their own even in an eating-house during Lent." Jimmy looked at him strangely when he made that remark, "Tommy" he said slowly but firmly "we are in the middle of a revolution, nothing like that matters now, we're about to take part in an attack on the British Empire and all you're thinking about is days of fast and abstinence. Anyway we are soldiers of the Irish Republic and soldiers on their way to war are exempt from all that."

Tommy blushed, thinking how stupid he was to bring up such a matter at a time like this. Jimmy was right, he would have to start thinking of higher things than life in Kildangan. This day would go down in history. He would make it up to Jimmy in the next few days and show him that he was a true believer in their mission. When they had finished the meal, Jimmy got up abruptly and headed off the kitchen to pay. On his return he said gruffly to Tommy "We'd better be heading off now if we want to make Dublin Town before morning."

One of the men at the counter looked up and gave the two of them a funny look. Maybe he was suspicious, thought Tommy or maybe Jimmy was misjudging the distance to Dublin. The city wasn't that far. Wicklow

people were famous for being nosey, maybe that was it.
Anyway they headed out and mounted the tired nag
who was now a bit refreshed from the rest and feed
from the nosebag.
They headed out the Brittas road. It was bitterly cold
now and they felt heavy after the meal. As soon as they
got out of the town, they stopped and relieved
themselves. Tommy was thinking about how lovely it
would have been to stay in the Slaney Arms and have a
few pints in front of the fire, but they could hardly win
a revolution that way.

"I'm going to leave the horse with a friend in Brittas"
announced Jimmy, "I don't think she can go much
further." It was true, the horse was beat and only
dragging herself along under the weight of the two men
and the tiredness of moving since early morning. It
seemed to take hours to get to the village of Brittas and
when they did it seemed as if everyone had retired for
the night. A few miserable flashes of candlelight or
firelight glimmered from the cottage windows.
The two-storied houses were completely dark but then
the kitchens were always at the back of these. On the
far side of the village they came to the forge which had
a single storey, slated house next door. "This is it" said
Jimmy as he dismounted. The top of the half-door
opened and a big, red-haired man with a ruddy
complexion about their own age greeted them. Tommy
gathered that he was a blacksmith just like Jimmy.
"You're good and early, come on in and warm
yourselves, I'll put the horse in the field behind. Come
on in now out of the cold and the Missus will give you

some tay."
Inside they seated themselves beside a roaring fire and the smiling Mrs Butler was already scalding the teapot from the kettle that hung on the crane over the fire.
"Wicked cold night to be on the road and you pair all the way from the south of Kildare, you must be perishing."
"We are indeed Mam, but we will soon warm up by your welcoming fireside" said Tommy, his spirits lifting at thoughts of a lovely warm cup of tea. When Micky, her husband, returned from putting away the horse, he joined them. "You had no trouble on the road I hope?"
"Divil a bit," replied Jimmy. "All's quiet, the plan of surprise seems to be working well, this is Tommy Brennan that I told you about, now a fully fledged member of the Brotherhood. We used to be comrades together in the Crimee." "I won't hold that against you" Micky smiled as he extended his hand of friendship to Tommy.
Tommy clasped it firmly and smiled back. This was a warm-hearted and friendly man, he could tell by his snug house and welcoming wife, but he was a bit alarmed by the way Jimmy had mentioned "the plan" in front of her. She must be in on the campaign as well, though he had never imagined such a thing as a woman Fenian, if not it was a funny way to keep secret. Nevertheless the warmth and comfort of the house and the friendliness of the welcome from the Butlers soothed him. For the first time all day he felt relaxed.

It was not to last long however. Tommy felt that he had

barely settled in and felt the glow of the fire mix with the warmth in his belly from the hot tea when Micky Butler abruptly ended it all. "Time to go, men" he announced, "There's work to be done this night." With that the three rose to their feet and from a press beside the dresser he took out three long bundles wrapped on sacking and tied with binder twine. "Lee Enfield rifles, only in from America, all greased and ready for use" he said. Without another word he handed them out along with a box each of ballcartridges.

Micky then turned to his wife and said "I'll see you in a few days or a week, Mary".

She stared at him blankly, all expression draining from her face. The three men walked silently out the door and into the dark, cold night. Mary, grabbing a bottle of Holy Water from the dresser, ran behind sprinkling some of the water over the departing men.

"May God bless and protect you all" she shouted after them. She stood watching for awhile as the men walked down the road with their suspicious looking bundles tucked under their arms. Then shivering in the bitter night she returned inside and closed and bolted the door.

Chapter 9

The Green Flag of Erin

The Battle of Tallaght

Evening of 5th March 1867

They were on their way to war just as surely as they had been back years ago when they marched through the Crimea to fight the soldiers of the Tsar. It was a freezing cold night with more snow threatening. Tommy didn't know where he was heading except for its name "Tallaght Hill" that Jimmy had divulged to him in the Public House in Baltinglass. He figured that is was somewhere in Dublin county way out from the city and in the foothills of the mountains maybe. Micky Butler had now taken charge and Tommy felt more confidence in his command than in that of the hot-headed, always-in-trouble Jimmy, whom he considered to be more of a foot soldier like himself than an officer. "Its about and hour's march from here, too dark and hilly to take a horse, we're better off on foot" Micky announced, answering an unspoken question in Tommy's head. "When do we link up with the others in the army?" asked Jimmy.
"They've been coming out from Dublin all evening, most should be in position on Tallaght Hill by 10 O'clock. From there we'll take all the Police Stations in the south of the county. By morning we will be at the

outskirts of Dublin and sweep the place like a new broom."

They walked on out the road from Brittas in the direction of Tallaght. At first there wasn't a soul to be seen, nor did they expect any except those who might be about the same business as themselves. It was a well kept secret alright or else there would have been police or military in evidence.

"Mr James Stephens will be the President of Ireland by this time tomorrow, just like they have a President in America" Jimmy optimistically announced. James Stephens was the leader of the Fenians and was called "The Head Centre" of this secret organisation and would become the first President of the Irish Republic. So Jimmy had told him boastfully and indiscreetly even before he had joined up. "There will be a provisional government established straightaway. When the war is over there will be elections for the whole country. From tomorrow Ireland will be ruled by Irishmen for the first time in hundreds of years, free from foreign domination."

"I think there might be a bit of fighting to be done before that Jimmy my boy" said Micky. "The British Army will send thousands of troops into the country when they wake up to find out what has happened, not to talk of the troops they already have in barracks here. I think this is going to be a long and bloody war." "And will we get help from abroad like in the old days in our history?" asked Tommy. "We will depend on what we can do for ourselves mainly but the Yanks will supply guns and generals, they have no time for the British at all after them supporting the Confederate States in the Civil War." "I didn't know that" said Tommy "I thought they stayed out of it".

"Well to all appearances they did but they wanted the Southern States to win and they slave owners and all, it had to do with trade in cotton. They supplied cotton to England for half nothing, that's all the British government was interested in."

"I think many of the landlords and the better-offs will support the government, even the Catholic ones, they don't like rebellion,"

"We'll deal with them when the war is over. Good landlords will have nothing to fear from the new republic, in fact we'll make laws to support them. But too many of them have been living a life of luxury on the backs of their tenants, evicting them when times get hard and letting their estates run down. The worst are of all are the absentee landlords, living it up in London while their tenants live in squalor and indeed in hunger itself or did so until recently".

Tommy was silent for awhile. He knew what Micky said was true and that good landlords like the More O'Ferralls and the O'Reillys before them were rarities but he felt protective of the More O'Ferralls who had such a good relationship with his family.

He was a bit embarrassed by it but he wasn't going to let his family down. "Not all landlords are bad" he said quietly.

"No" said Micky" and we will make sure that good landlords don't suffer, we're not trying to take the land off them. Only those who won't accept the Republic will be our enemies, it's been all worked out by the men who founded the movement and who run it from America."

By now they were meeting other small groups of men on the road. It seemed as if a steady stream were heading for Tallaght Hill. Most carried bundles in all shapes and sizes. Jimmy was mystified as to the contents of some bundles, by their shapes they certainly weren't guns. "Some of them are carrying supplies" said Micky, yet again answering a question by Tommy before he had time to put it. Each group acknowledged the other and chatted away as if they were going to a fair or a wake.

After an hour they came to Jobstown Cross where the lights of Mr Clarke's Public House beckoned them. "We might as well warm up in here before the night ahead" suggested Micky. Tommy and Jimmy didn't need any encouragement and eagerly followed Micky in the door of the tavern. What they saw inside amazed them. The small pub was packed tight with men, there must have been forty or so jammed into the small room. Some had moved into the private rooms of the house while Mr Clarke happily pulled pint after pint and liberal measures of whiskey for this unexpectedly large crowd. The customers were in small groups chatting and laughing together. Nobody gave more than a passing look to the three men who had just walked in. Micky moved to the counter leaving Jimmy and Tommy behind to wait for him to return with the pints. Jimmy" said Tommy" I don't like this, I thought we were heading for a revolution, not a drinking session." Now it was Jimmy's turn to be embarrassed. "These

men were never in the army, they need a bit of Dutch courage, that's all, they'll only be here for one or two."
"By the looks of some of them, they're here for the night." Jimmy looked around him and back at Tommy who could see the anger in his eyes. When Micky returned he confirmed their worst fears about what was happening.
"These men are supposed to be on Tallaght Hill by this time. A fellow at the bar told me they were tired after walking all the way from Dublin. It's only seven or eight miles. The fellow was a captain and he is leading the drinking. Some bloody use he will be on the battlefield. Let's finish up and head for the hill."
"There's bound to be thousands more up there by now" suggested Tommy reassuringly.
They lowered their pints in double quick time and before they headed out Micky returned to the bar and raising his voice above the din proclaimed "You're a bloody disgrace to the republic Captain, get these men up to the hill".
The Captain glared at him and replied "Fuck off Ginger, get back to the bog where you came from" His comrades all around him broke into a loud, laughing cheer. Tommy was more than a bit surprised when Micky walked away without a word, if it was Jimmy he would have the hit the man a box. Micky was a man of discipline, thought Tommy, able to control his temper even when he was insulted like this. He knew there were higher things at stake. The three men walked out to the laughter and derision of the customers at the counter.

In the chill night air they followed Micky in silence down the road towards Tallaght village. A dark mood settled over the three of them. Soon the presence of other small groups on the road restored their spirits somewhat but still they didn't speak. After about a mile of trudging the dim lights of Tallaght village came into view. As they neared the village they heard the crackling sound of firearms. "Time to ready your weapons men, I think we're about to see some action" said Micky with a bit of certainty creeping back into his voice. They unfurled the sacking from their rifles and discarded it by the roadside. Tommy and Jimmy loaded their guns in double quick time like they had learned so long ago. They were now in clear sight of the twenty of so houses making up the village of Tallaght.

Right in the middle stood the police barracks from which they could see the flashes of volley after volley of rifle shot. From here and there in front of and around the house came sporadic replies. Men were running up and down the street shouting at one another. Some were running past the barracks and shooting wildly as they ran with no chance of aiming properly or hitting anything. There seemed to be no rank that surrounded the house to subject it to sustained fire, only sporadic replies to the well-aimed shots from the barracks. Several men passed them abandoning the fight and heading back up Jobstown Road instead of north to Tallaght Hill. "This is not part of the plan. Its not supposed to start here" Micky said angrily. "We're supposed to be on the hill where we will make formation, let's skirt around the village and head for the hill. It'll be a different picture we'll see there, this looks

like a god-awful mess."
Bypassing the village they headed out the road again in the direction of their rendezvous at Tallaght Hill. "The roof on that barracks was thatch, why didn't they set fire to it?" asked Tommy. "Because they don't know their arse from their elbow" replied Jimmy who hadn't spoken for some time and now seemed fit to explode with suppressed anger.
"Listen" said Micky, "Not a shot was to be fired until we reached the hill where we are to be put into brigades and fan out all over the south of the county. Some bloody hotheads must have taken it into their heads to attack the police station on the way. Now the Polis from all over Dublin County will be alerted and the soldiers too. Dublin City is full of soldiers and we were not supposed to come up against them till we had secured the rural areas. I don't know what the hell is going to happen now, we'll make for the hill anyway and take our orders from there."

It was only a half hour's march from the village to Tallaght Hill, but the going was slow on account of the snow on the ground which was heavier here as they were heading uphill. Other groups were heading up there too but worryingly some seemed to be moving in the opposite direction.
One lad shouted at them "No point in going up there" or something like that through the cold night's air. They were mystified by his remarks and ignored him. They carried on. They turned up a side road which was really a narrow track or bohereen, Micky knew his way alright. By now more men were heading away from the

hill than towards it though there was no rush, just walking away. It all seemed so casual. Maybe, Tommy thought to himself, these men were being sent somewhere by the commanders on the hill. The hill itself was an ancient place where the pagans buried their dead even before the time of St Patrick. It was a good hill and would be easy to defend, really a foothill to the Dublin mountains. All of south county Dublin lay to the north. It was an excellent choice to sweep through the county and into the city. In spite of its ancient ceremonial past it was now just an enormous scrubby field, part of a farm. They entered through an open gate. There were groups of men standing around chatting. Very few seemed to be armed and the glow of their pipes visible all over the field and beyond.

In the middle of the field on a makeshift flagpole hung the green flag of Erin with thirty-two stars on it made out in gold embroidery. But there was no one beside it, no commander at a fold-away table giving orders as they expected. Just a lonely flag fluttering in the half dark evening. The gathering was not like an army as Jimmy and Tommy were used to from their days in the Crimea. It was more like the prelude to a fair or a pilgrimage.
"You two just wait here, I'll see what's going on" instructed Micky. "I don't like this set up one bloody bit" said Jimmy when Micky was just out of earshot. "Seems like a massive balls-up, if you ask me, nobody seems to know what's going on." "And where are the American officers? Nobody is in charge, this is a total mess, it's more like a fair than a army getting ready to

march" replied Tommy.
It wasn't that there weren't plenty of men around, there must have been hundreds just standing there waiting for something to happen or somebody with authority telling them what to do. But nothing was happening, just groups standing around chatting and smoking, some rubbing their hands and stamping their feet trying to keep warm in the cold night air. Now and then a shout would break out as if someone was trying to make order out of the chaos, but then it subsided and the different groups continued on in their harmless banter. As many were leaving as were coming in the gate and there seemed to be no central point for the men. There was no one to whom they were reporting or who was directing operations.
Just a thousand or so men, so it seemed to Tommy, standing around in a snow covered field, they might as well have been cattle. Seasoned soldiers like Jimmy and Tommy looked at one another in shocked and disgusted silence.

"What's going on at all?" Tommy enquired of a man standing near them. "Captain O'Donoghue and a cartload of arms were coming up the Rathfarnham road and were ambushed by the Polis, I think they shot and killed him, anyway they got the arms, I think we're in a bit of trouble, everything seems to have fallen to pieces here." "We've come up from Kildare, there's fighting in Tallaght at the barracks" "Yeah, I know, we passed it too, a few other barracks have been attacked as well all over the county. But the leaders all seem to have been captured on the way, there's nobody with any authority here, not even from the Executive, nobody knows what to do next".

Tommy wouldn't have known who was on the Fenian Executive anyway but maybe Jimmy who was listening in, would have.

He turned to him. "I don't think this is going to work out Jimmy boy." "Jesus, look at them" said Jimmy. "They're standing round looking like they're at a political meeting and waiting for someone to stand up and make a speech." He was raising his voice now and getting stares from the groups of men in the vicinity, though most of them seemed as bewildered as he was.

Just then Micky came striding over to them. "It's gone to pot" he said, "The captains have been captured on the way here, or at least none of them have turned up, everyone is waiting around for orders and there's no one to give them. What's wrong with you?" he asked of Jimmy.

Jimmy Dunne, veteran of the Crimea and hard man from Kildangan, stood beside them shaking with grief and anger as the tears rolled down his cheeks into his bushy brown beard. "Ten bloody years of work gone down the drain, we'll never live this down" he sobbed. Tommy didn't know if his friend was weeping from sadness at the lost Fenian cause or the fury and frustration of having been made a fool of, he certainly felt like a fool himself that night on Tallaght Hill. "Maybe it's working down the country, isn't the rising taking place all over Ireland tonight" he said reassuringly to his friend, though he didn't really believe it himself. If they couldn't get it right for Dublin where the Fenian Brotherhood was strongest, there was little chance that it would come together in the country areas. Echoing his thoughts, Jimmy said "It has to start in Dublin, we have to take the city and Dublin Castle, there are hundreds of cells in the city then the rest of the country follows our lead, if it fails in Dublin, it fails everywhere."

"What's to be done Micky?" Tommy asked. "Divil a thing" replied Micky. "We are only the foot soldiers, if we have no leaders and no arms there's nothing we can do. This thing is a disaster, can't you see that for yourselves? I think its time to get out of here before the polis or the soldiers arrive, pull yourself together Jimmy, there'll be another day for Ireland." "There will like fuck" said Jimmy and he threw his rifle on the ground where it clattered against a rock. Micky picked up the valuable piece of merchandise but made no comment and no attempt to hand it back to Jimmy.

"You can count me out after this and I mean it" he said in disgust. The three men trudged out the gate they had come in through only moments before and back downhill towards Tallaght village and the Brittas Road in silence.

The cold and their weariness gripped them as much as their disappointment and shattered dreams as they headed back for Micky's house in Brittas.

Chapter 10

The return of the prodigal son

It was the small hours of Thursday morning before Tommy got home to Kildangan. The miles home seemed to take days and Jimmy was morose and sulky all the way as if the failure of the revolution was a personal insult to him. He didn't say much except that he was getting out of Ireland. Tommy took it all rather philosophically, he knew from the moment that they entered the pub in Jobstown that the adventure was doomed. The men drinking there were just chancers and adventurers, filling themselves with porter when they were supposed to be marching to war. It was a joke. So what happened or rather what did not happen on Tallaght Hill was less of a surprise and a disappointment to him than it was to Jimmy. Now he just wanted to get home and resume his former life. For him it was all over, it was only a childish dream anyway.
"There's no hope for this country, the people have no respect for themselves" Jimmy said again and again. "They deserve to be under the heel of the British Empire, they are just born to be slaves." Tommy was more concerned about getting back to his cosy homestead, his wife and family. The authorities must be searching for stragglers from Tallaght, they reckoned.

So they avoided the villages or any houses they could so that they wouldn't be spotted as they headed for Brittas. When they arrived at Micky's house, they had a bite to eat, his friendly wife gave them a feed of bacon and calcannon. She remained silent when Micky told her of the disastrous end to the rising. She didn't seem surprised at all. Tommy felt a bit guilty about taking the food as he hadn't forgotten that it was now Lent. He would make up for it in some other way. God would make an exception. It wasn't everyday that there was a revolution going on, even if it was a botched one. Surely there must be a dispensation for revolutionaries, for Catholic ones at least, he thought. When he settled back home he would go to Confession over the Oath, that should be alright. He had taken it under duress and the priest would understand.

After the feed in Brittas they had nodded off by the fire for half an hour before they bade goodbye to Micky and his friendly wife. They wouldn't stay any longer as they knew that if they were caught there they would get Micky into even more trouble. He was surely a known rebel in the area and it would only be a matter of time before the Constabulary came knocking on his door and enquiring as to his movements that night. The presence of two men there would have given the game away. Anyway they knew that Micky and his wife were glad to see them go. They had their own life to protect as well.

Jimmy had lost all his spirits even though he had tucked in to the dinner. He didn't seem to care about anything anymore and just tagged along, for the first time in his life giving into Tommy's wishes. They had left the horse behind too, Tommy thought Jimmy might object to that as a horse was a very valuable item and he was bound to get into trouble with his father if he returned without it. But even here he conceded. Micky told him he could retrieve it in a few days or even weeks when things quietened down. Tommy decided that they must skirt around the towns and villages. Walking through the snow covered fields was no problem to these country boys, even in the dark which would last for a few more hours more. They had done it all their lives and would have enjoyed it if it weren't for their tiredness and low spirits and for Tommy at least, sickness in his stomach about what would happen next and his own stupidity.

Would he be able to resume his former life just like that or had he ruined everything and face dismissal from his position in More O'Ferrall's yard? What has he done to Julia and his family? Maybe jail or emigration at the best were facing him. For the remainder of the night and all the following day, they trudged through the fields and woods of Kildare, heading for the south. Now and then they saw men working in the fields but didn't stop even to bid them good day. It was like those enormous marches they made in the Crimea

Tommy Brennan in 1870

All day they walked, weary and hungry but they never faltered for a moment, only stopping for a break every few hours but never lying down or sleeping. They knew their future depended on their getting home as soon as possible.

It was well after midnight when he tapped lightly on the window of the bedroom of his own house in Kildangan. He had been away for almost two days, moving all the time with only a short sleep in Micky Butler's house the night before.
He was sick with exhaustion and worry about being captured on the way home.
He could never have explained the reason for being out so late, wandering around the country and maybe he would face jail or transportation and loose everything that was dear to him. How could he have been so foolish? To his relief Julia answered immediately as if she was expecting him, as indeed she was. When he saw her framed in the doorway, her beauty and the warmth escaping from the house hit him like a bolt. Immediately he wanted her as he never wanted her before, even on their wedding night. "Thank God you're back safe" she whispered after she had quietly unbolted the door. She stood there in her long white night-dress and her hair loose about her head and her breasts protruding clearly. Oh God! How he loved those dugs, so pointy and firm. There she stood looking sweetly at him as if he had just been away at a fair, not one word or look of reproach for his desertion.
For a moment he was transfixed by what he saw. She looked so beautiful then, never had he seen such a

welcome sight. A Republic would be grand, he thought but there was no place like home and no woman like Julia. She led him through the warm kitchen with her finger to her lips urging him to move silently lest he wake his parents. The kitchen was so warm and welcoming to Tommy and faintly lit by the embers of the fire in the grate as they moved silently into the new room which was their bedroom. Tommy had removed his boots at the door and in his stocking feet he moved as quietly as possible, hardly believing that it was all over and that he was heading into bed with his wife.

He would have a lot of explaining to do to his parents who were sleeping in their room on the other side of the kitchen. The children slumbered soundly in the other bed as Julia helped her man off with his clothes. "They think you're sick up at the Yard, Daddy said you had a fever" she whispered. "I'm glad to be home Julia" was all Tommy said before he stretched on the bed in his long johns and vest. He wanted to say more but couldn't think of what words to use but he knew Julia would understand what was in his head and left unsaid.
Then she pulled the covers over him and got in beside him. He took her in his arms and his exhaustion disappeared and his sex instinct took over as if he had no control over it at all. He pulled up her nightdress and fondled her gorgeous breasts. He didn't even care if he woke the children, something that he was usually very careful about. He didn't even care if his parents heard him, so violent and urgent were his desires. It didn't take him long to climax, so heightened was his arousal. When he had finished he felt weary and drained in

every bone and muscle of his body but oh so happy, fulfilled and satisfied. Here was where he belonged: with his lovely wife in his warm bed. Julia's sparkling eyes showed she was expecting some more from him but smiled indulgently as her husband closed his eyes and fell into a sleep of exhaustion and satisfaction.

His head only seemed to have hit the pillow when he awoke with a fright to his mother shaking him. He stared at her and jerked up in the bed. "Its alright pet, you're home" she said soothingly.
"Daddy is in the kitchen waiting for you, better shake yourself, its near time to head up to the yard". Feeling jaded and sore all over Tommy pulled on his clothes. Julia was not in the bedroom and must have arisen earlier. He went to the kitchen where his father, with his head down, was eating a bowl of stirabout. Tommy sat opposite him and Julia laid a bowl in front of him. "Fitzgerald, the bastard, knows there's something up. You're to look sick and shook as if you've been in bed since Monday night, that's what I told him. It would be a feather in his cap to get you fired. It would get back at me and this family. Don't let him get the better of us. No matter what he says, keep cool. Mr More O'Ferrall is a good man but if his mind has been poisoned by that rat about you being out with the rebels and all, there's no knowing what he might do. He's a great believer in the law. Finish up your breakfast quickly now and we'll head in that bit early and find the lay of the land, remember son, there's a lot hanging on this and not only your own position" Father and son looked at one another across the table and Tommy realised for the

first time that it was not only his own future that was at stake but his father's and his family.

"We could be put out on the road over this and end up in the poorhouse." He spoke slowly and softly without looking at his wife or daughter-in-law. He was speaking directly to his son.
"I won't let you down Daddy" Tommy said. It was a chill spring's morning when the two men headed up to the estate yard and it was still fairly dark. It was as hard a walk for Tommy as his one home from Tallaght Hill the day and night before, he was stiff all over and nervous about the coming confrontation. Thank God he had told no one of his destination or there would have been no point in returning here. It had all been Jimmy's idea and he had let himself be led into it like a gobshite. The clock in the yard showed a quarter to six. The supervisor, Fitzgerald was on the go, walking around and waiting for the bell to ring at six and that the men were all about their tasks immediately after. "Sharp morning, Mr Fitzgerald" his father saluted him and Fitzgerald spun round, his face scowling when he saw Tommy. "I thought we'd seen the last of you" he said. "Only a touch of the fever, sir" Tommy replied. "I feel great again, something I picked up in the Crimee, it comes at me now and again."

Tommy had hit a sore point with supervisor. He had not sent his son to fight in the Crimea and resented the fact that Willy Brennan had, thereby gaining the gratitude and respect of Mr More O'Ferrall. He could see a warning look come over his father's face. Antagonising

Fitzgerald mightn't be the cleverest of tactics at this stage. "Right, get to work, there's no point standing around here all day chatting. Clean out the byre, the milkmaids should be here by now, Willy, attend to the horses."

The two men headed off leaving the supervisor with a bitter look on his face.

Tommy was delighted to be back at work. Though it had only been Monday last since he had been in the yard he felt that it had been ages. Every muscle in his body ached as he wielded the fork to clean away the dung from the cowhouse and load it into the wheelbarrow for transportation to the dung heap at the back of the byre. It was nice and familiar in the cowhouse and the smell of warm animals and their dung felt very comforting and re-assuring. What had gotten into his head he wondered, to risk all this for an adventure with that eejit Jimmy Dunne?

An Irish Republic would be grand but he would still end up shovelling dung for the More O'Ferralls, republic or no republic. If he got out of this he would settle down with his wife and family. Who could ask for more and how could he have been so stupid as to jeopardise it?

A grand wife and two healthy sons, a fine roof over his head and his father and mother in good health, it was enough to make him kick himself at his own foolishness.

Just as he was finishing up, Fitzgerald walked into the byre. He looked around as if to see that Tommy was doing his work diligently and then with a complacent

look on his face said gruffly "Brennan, please attend on Mr More O'Ferrall after his ride. Wait for him in the stables."
With that he turned and left. In spite of his attempts to hide it, Tommy thought he detected a smirk on Fitzgerald's face. So this was it, thought Tommy, a face to face with Mr More O'Ferrall. Was he now to lose his position, would his father be fired too, would his whole family be driven off the estate? Mr O'Ferrall had been High Sheriff of Kildare in 1856 and was a stickler for the law. There was no chance he would countenance an act of rebellion or employ those who did on his estate. This was the end of the road. He would go to America and join his Uncle Nicholas there. It was all his own doing and he didn't feel guilty about it, the Irish had a right to rule their own country.
He was not ashamed of joining the Fenians, only embarrassed about how daft and badly organised the whole thing was, but it was wrong to take it out on his whole family. If only he could save his father's position, it was damned unfair that he would be punished too. And their lovely house, would they be turfed out of the homestead where they had lived for generations?
There was a lot riding on this interview with Mr More O'Ferrall.

It had been Charles More O'Ferrall's custom to ride for an hour each morning before breakfast. Now that he had passed the sixty mark he allowed himself just half of that. He was a lucky man to have his health at that age and he thanked God for it every day. All his life had been blessed by providence and good fortune. The fifth son of an ancient, landed family who had barely kept the wolf from the door in the past fifty years though they had kept most of their estates and position during the years of the Penal Laws. During that time many Catholic families had gone to the wall. As the fifth son he had no prospects of a family inheritance and the colonial service or the Church didn't appeal to him, so he was facing a bleak future. That was until Susan O'Reilly accepted his proposal of marriage. Through her he had had come into the estate at Kildangan and an estate in Mayo, God help us. She had given him a fine healthy son, Dominick, though she had passed away in childbirth. Dominick was now away at school with the Jesuits at Clongowes Wood College, the same school he had attended himself and the leading school for Catholic gentry. She was his own saint in heaven, he prayed for her intercession every day.

Today as he did the rounds of his estate he had much on his mind. Accompanied by his favourite dog, Bran, a brown retriever, running beside his horse and sitting straight as a die on his mount and wearing his top hat, he made an impressive figure. Though he enjoyed his morning ride, he knew it was important also to be seen around his estate, it connected him to his workers and tenants. He was proud of the relationship he had with his people and that he was known as a good landlord. It also gave him time to think about the oncoming day and the problems and choices facing him.
He had to clear the Brennans off his estate, he would pay for the passage for them to America or maybe the

Argentine. Irish people of farming stock seemed to be doing well there. Fitzgerald had told him that the yardman Thomas had been out with the Fenians in that disgraceful episode in Dublin County. He couldn't shelter a nest of rebels on his estate. By upholding the law, he and his family had done much for the Catholic cause in Ireland.

He had been High Sheriff of Kildare, the highest post a Catholic in the county had achieved since the Reformation. It was conferred on him by the Queen herself, and his uncle had been Governor of Malta some years back. He had resigned over the Ecclesiastical Titles Bill, a piece of stupid English bigotry which had denied the Pope the right to appoint bishops to English Sees as he had done since the time of St Peter. He had done the right thing then and would do the right thing now, though it was hard to dismiss a family like the Brennans who had served Susan and her family right back to the previous century and indeed served himself well.

He remembered that they had sent their son to fight in the Crimea when he had appealed to his tenants and staff for volunteers. That son was the one that was the cause of the present trouble. He was not afraid to make a hard decision if he knew it was the right one. These thoughts filled the head of Charles More O'Ferrall as he cantered around his lands on that Thursday morning.

Young Brennan was a brave lad though, it was no small thing to risk everything for an idea. That was what he had done himself all his life, and the lad held the Crimean War medal and to all the locals he was known as "Crimee Tommy" because of his service there. In these parts they couldn't get their tongues around the "ea" sound, funny the accents of the peasantry! He wondered if it was the same in England. That medal was a badge of honour. What would Susan have said if she was at his side that morning as rode through her beloved demesne?

What indeed? Now he remembered a remark made to him by the Lord Chief Justice, Thomas Lefroy when he had resigned from the position of High Sheriff of Kildare. "Resigning is in your blood. More O'Ferrall" he had sneered, referring to his uncle Richard who had resigned from the position of Governor of Malta many years previously.

That remark really rankled and had made him twitch with anger though he had tried hard to conceal it. It still rankled. These government appointed judges did not understand or appreciate men of principle no more than the English did. Anyway, who the hell was Lefroy anyway? It sounded like one of those Huguenots who came over from France only a few generations ago, expelled by their own king. Who was he to talk down to the More O'Ferralls who could trace their lineage back a thousand years to the O'Moores, the lords of Leix in Queen's County.

Maybe he should have stayed on as High Sheriff, the whole controversy over the Ecclesiastical Titles Bill had blown over and though passed by Parliament had never been put into force. The English Catholics now had their own bishops appointed by his Holiness. There would have been serious consequences if the Bill had been enforced.

The Liberal Party would never have had another Member of Parliament elected in Ireland again, at least not outside of Ulster or Dublin. He would face his responsibilities, he wouldn't expect Fitzgerald the overseer to do it for him, he was the landowner and wouldn't shirk his duty. Land ownership had its duties as well as its privileges as Mr Drummond, the Chief Secretary had said many years ago. Pity though that young Brennan was a Crimean War veteran. He had been able to hold his head up high among the other members of the gentry because so many young men from his estates had gone off to the Crimea to fight for Queen and country.

Those bloody Fenians, he thought, leading young men astray and running around the country like a rabble. They hadn't one gentleman amongst them. They were nothing but a crowd of illiterates, apprentices, tradesmen and ragamuffins like those impious Italians who were threatening the Pope out of his own territories, the Papal States which had been handed down to him through the generations by the Emperor Constantine. Ireland's wrongs could be righted by parliamentary and legal means, without bloodshed and led by gentleman like himself or professional men like Daniel O'Connell, not by a crowd of tradesmen like the Fenians. Yet there was a nagging doubt in his mind. What if they had succeeded? A country run by blacksmiths and carpenters? There was little chance of that and anyway Ireland's future lay within the Empire. It was a great pity that Thomas Brennan had been

dragged into all this, a good and brave young man and from a family that had always been loyal to the estate, to him and to his wife's family over the years.
When he reached the stable Tommy Brennan was waiting for him as he had been instructed to by Mr. Fitzgerald

"Good Morning Mr. More O'Ferrall" said Tommy touching his forelock as he took the horse's bridle. Bran ran up to Tommy and yelped and wagged his tail in recognition. Charles dismounted with a grunt and a great effort. He wasn't getting any younger and the stiffness of old age was what he hated most.
"I believe you have been away from your duties for the last few days Brennan" he said when he had regained his footing and looking into the distance beyond his worker. "Yes Sir" replied Tommy "I have been down with a fever, Sir, something I caught in the Crimee, it comes at me now and again, I'm as right as rain now."
"A fever was it?" said More O'Ferrall still looking into the distance beyond Tommy's right shoulder, "Maybe it was, there seems to be a fever running through the country at the moment, a very dangerous fever in fact."
Then he looked straight into Tommy's eyes and Tommy felt the stare directly. He winced and wanted to look away but knew he must look the other man directly in the eyes.
"Tell me Brennan, are you cured of this fever now or is it likely to re-occur? I couldn't have that around here, other men might catch it." "I'm completely cured of the fever Mr. More O'Ferrall, I give you my word on it, as sure as God is my judge." More O'Ferrall looked away.

"Well I'm very glad to hear it, my late wife was very attached to your family." With that he put his riding crop under his arm and headed for the house and breakfast. He turned as he went, crunching the gravel under his feet. "And Brennan make sure you're at eight o'clock Mass on Sunday morning." "Yes Sir" Tommy replied, his heart pounding in his breast and fit to burst, he could hardly believe that his ordeal was over.

Part II

The atmosphere in the Brennan household that day varied from one of terrifying foreboding to one of numbing relief. It was as if a death sentence had been lifted from them. Catherine and Julia had spent the whole morning praying for their men and the family's future in Kildangan. They were only to know the outcome when Tommy and Willy came in for dinner after one o'clock, though they knew the worst had passed by eight or nine in the morning as the men would have returned to the house by then if they had been dismissed, but they couldn't be completely sure till the men returned. The dinner was eaten in subdued relief as Tommy repeated word for word what Mr More O'Ferrall's had said to him.
"Thank God for the More O'Ferralls" said his father "There's some dacency left in Ireland, and there's no dacency like old dacency".
"Thank God for the Lady, its her who's looking after this family today, I've been praying to her all morning" Catherine had said, sounding almost as if she were correcting her husband, which she was in a way. "You mean Our Lady?" her husband asked, knowing that she meant no such thing. "No" replied Catherine "I mean, the Lady Susan O'Reilly, she's the one who got us off, she is in heaven looking after the Brennans." "Well anyway" her husband chuckled" Fitzgerald must be fuming"
"What's this about going to eight o'clock mass on Sunday?" asked Tommy, genuinely perplexed. "You

are going to be read off the altar, it'll be a disgrace for the family but it's better than losing your job and us being put out on the road" his mother said.

"The priests should keep their noses out of politics" his father mused.

"It will be a shame on the whole family, it will be remembered for generations" Julia his wife, interjected. There was a shocked silence around the table: Tommy couldn't believe that his own wife had come out with such a statement. "Taking the Fenian oath is a mortal sin, the Church is against secret societies" she added as if she hadn't said enough already.

"A sin" Willy interjected "What the hell is going on here? They seem to be inventing a new sin every day." But it was Julia who had won the argument.

When they returned to work, the men didn't mention Julia's comments but it affected Tommy deeply. All the good feeling he had about his interview with More O'Ferrall disappeared. What was it all about? He thought Julia of all people had understood his actions, it seemed to him that she was taking a stand against him. It wasn't just that he felt that she had betrayed him, it was that she didn't understand, she was on a different track to him entirely. He felt as alone as he did in the Crimea surrounded by bloodthirsty men.

Maybe he hadn't explained himself to her, that must be it, sometimes he didn't explain things to others, he took it for granted that they saw things as he did or in the case of some men, he didn't care if they understood or not. But he had felt that Julia would understand without an explanation, now he saw that there was a distance between them that he had never seen before. He spent the whole afternoon thinking about it but didn't mention it to her when he got home though he had planned to do so. He just bottled it up inside himself.

On Friday evening Tommy's father had furnished himself with a copy of the Freeman's Journal. Tommy longed to find out what was in the paper about the rising and to see what it said about the affair at Tallaght Hill and what had happened in the rest of the country. There had been no talk of it up in the yard on Thursday, most didn't know anything like that was happening outside of Kildangan and those who did probably suspected that Tommy's story of his two days in bed with the fever were a yarn and kept their mouths shut to keep him out of trouble. However he learned that Jimmy Dunne, the blacksmith's son had left home and that everyone believed he was out with the Fenians. On Friday it was a different matter, news of his interview with Mr More O'Ferrall had spread like wildfire though nobody had mentioned it to his face. When the family gathered round the fire that Friday night Willy Brennan finally opened up the paper and handed it to his son.

"Read that bit out loud" he said pointing to the Editorial. Tommy read out aloud to the expectant household,
"The accounts received from the provinces, through our Special Correspondents are, on the whole reassuring and leave little room for doubting that the wicked and irresponsible □rising of the Fenians has been effectively suppressed."

"I don't see why you have to get the boy to read all this," interrupted Catherine, "hasn't he been through enough already?" "We've all been through a lot, woman, and anyway he's not a boy anymore" her husband replied, "and now we want to know what the Journal thinks of it all. We might even learn something from it, read on Tommy." "We only know that it was not a general uprising, that there was a remarkable absence of the leaders, that not one of the Fenian Uniforms, much less of the Generals, Field Officers or even Captains who own them, appeared in the field, that the arms were not brought out, that the rifles that ☐sniffed the morning air could be counted by dozens, that the pikemakers could produce in one week every pike that was captured, or even seen and that in areas where Fenianism is most potent there was no rising."

"I think" said the old man "that the paper is right, it was mad and wicked, isn't that what they said, there's no point fighting the English, their army is too strong, surely an army man like you know that, Tommy, after the Crimee and all." "I do now" conceded his son "but they could have put up some fight, the whole thing was a shambles, the police broke the whole thing up, they didn't even need to bring out the army." "Maybe the next time a bit more thought should be put into it, anyway the Irish never got anywhere without a strong leader. That's what I don't understand, there was no leader in the field, they say that James Stephens has gone to France" said his father as he lit his pipe. Tommy started to read again but silently now as he learned of the collapse of the rising all over the country in just one week.

Epilogue

On Sunday the estate workers and their families attended eight o'clock mass. This gave them time to do whatever work in the yard that was absolutely necessary on the Sunday morning without breaking the Sabbath prohibition on manual labour and then after that they were free for the rest of the day.
The little chapel at Kildangan was packed as usual. At the front, in the family seat and all alone sat Charles Edward More O'Ferrall. As the local landowner and patron of the church he was always there half an hour before the Mass began. That was partly from courtesy because the service would never begin until he arrived and also because he savoured this time when he was left completely alone. No one would ever disturb him as he knelt before the altar of his own church. Today as he prayed mechanically, he pondered on his decision to turn a blind eye to young Brennan's participation in the Fenian rising of the week gone by. Looking back, it had been a harmless enough event with the police breaking up the few attempts at insurrection and a mopping up operation being carried out particularly in the snow covered countryside of Munster. Maybe that would be the end of it all now and the country would settle down. At the next election, under the new Franchise Act every man would have a vote, maybe that would make a change in the quality of Irish representation at the Westminster Parliament and the Fenians would wither away, this is what he thought and hoped would happen. He prayed they would all leave Kildangan alone, it was

a prosperous and happy place under his stewardship
and it was his duty to make sure it remained so.
He was glad he let young Brennan off, he was just a
young man led astray by his own enthusiasm and love
of adventure. It was partly his own fault, sending him
off to the Crimea all those years back and seeing what
the world outside Ireland was like.
When men got a taste of adventure and foreign places it
was very hard for them to settle down again, especially
in a quiet place like Kildangan where nothing seemed
to happen except the change in the seasons and the
natural rhythms of births, deaths and marriages.
Anyway he wasn't going to be told who to employ and
who not to employ on his own estates by a crowd of
second rate English pen pushers in Dublin Castle. They
knew nothing about Ireland and cared less except that it
was a handy meal ticket for them. He felt absolutely
confident that he knew from his prayers that Susan
approved of what he had done.

At eight o'clock precisely the altar bells rang and six
boys in long black soutanes covered by shorter white
surplices walked out of the sacristy. The congregation
in the church hushed immediately and stood up.
The servers were followed by the Parish Priest of
Monasterevin, Fr Michael Ryan, into which area
Kildangan fell. He was a small jolly looking man with a
slightly protuberant belly and a youthful face with rosy
cheeks which betrayed his love of a few whiskeys
before bed each night. He was a Tipperary South
Riding man and thus a Munsterman. This annoyed his
fellow priests even more as they coveted the prosperous

and quiet parish of Monastrevin at the heart of Leinster. They put it down to Fr. Ryan's relationship with the late bishop whose mother's maiden name was Ryan. Just another case of nepotism, appointing his nephew to a cushy parish, they murmured knowingly and jealously to one another. Fr. Ryan was fully committed to the new trends in the Church which worked at bringing it into full obedience to Rome. He had no time for the semi-independent status of the older bishops and priests and their tolerance of the ancient pagan customs of the lower classes like their drunken fairs and pilgrimages. His great hero was Archbishop Paul Cullen of Dublin who had been made a Cardinal the previous year and was a Kildare man to boot. He was the great moderniser of the Irish Church and had the full support of the Pope. In spite of his jovial appearance, Father Ryan ruled his curates and his parishioners with a rod of iron.

Mr More O'Ferrall knew him well and thoroughly approved of his orthodoxy. Indeed, he had officiated at his marriage to Susan some eighteen years previously. It was unusual for the Parish Priest himself to read the 8 o'clock mass on Sunday in a small place like Kildangan and his appearance sent a silent shudder through the congregation as Mr More O'Ferrall knew it would. There was something special afoot and the congregation knew it. It was exciting and terrifying for them at the same time.

The priest's highly polished black boots appeared from under the long flowing white robe called the Alb. Over this he wore the embroidered silk vestments, coloured

purple as a sign of penitence as was laid down by
Canon Law for the holy season of Lent. At the
centre of the cross on the back was embroidered in gold
sequins the Greek letters IHS. On his head he wore the
black four-cornered hat called a biretta and in his right
hand he held the ciborium or cup, full of the as yet
unconsecrated bread. It too was dressed in purple.
Though he was not a tall man, he had an air of
importance and that, added to the splendour of his
vestments made him a very imposing figure of
authority. The altarboys lined up in perfect precision as
the bottom of the altar steps, three on each side and the
priest stood between them, all facing the altar with their
backs to the congregation. He removed his biretta and
handed it to the server on his right. "Introibo ad altare
Dei" the priest bellowed and the servers shouted back
"A Deam qui laetificat juven tutem meam."
Charles read the English translation from his missal,
though he knew the meaning full well. "I will go unto
the altar of God, the God of my gladness and joy".
Then the priest ascended the three steps up to the altar.
The Mass had begun.

Tommy sat half way down the little church with his
parents, his wife Julia and his boys. Something had
changed between himself and Julia and not in a good
way, he felt distant from her. It was as if there had been
an amputation in their relationship since her outburst at
dinnertime on Thursday. He still desired her though,
she was a fine figure of a woman. His two sons, James
and Nicholas also sat in the pew, silent as usual. James
was thinking about a game of marbles he might play

with his schoolfriends after breakfast. Nicholas was the more sensitive and the more intelligent of the two and he sensed the tension all around him. Even before proceedings began he was ready to burst into tears. He sensed that something bad was going to happen. Sometimes Tommy would have stood at the back mixing and chatting in whispers with the hard men of the village but on this occasion he knew he had better be further up the chapel and to take part fully on today of all days and in the company of his family. Mr More O'Ferrall had made this quite clear to him. He knew the priests were against the Fenians and Jimmy Dunne had told him what Charles Kickham, the Tipperary Fenian leader and writer had said about them: "In the old days we had wooden chalices and golden priests, now we had golden chalices and wooden priests." That must have really gotten up their noses!

Still a deal was a deal and he had made a promise to Mr More O'Ferrall. The night before he had gone to Confession and told the priest of the Fenian Oath he had taken. It was a serious sin to belong to a secret oath-bound organisation and he was relieved when he was given absolution. Sometimes people had to go to the bishop for absolution in the case of sins like this. They were so serious that they were called reserved sins, not to be forgiven by ordinary priests but requiring confession and absolution from a bishop.
It was funny though he thought, it was not a sin to go out with the Fenians which the law considered to be treason but it was a serious sin to take the Oath which was afterall just a few words and a promise, that's all it

was to him anyway.

After the first gospel came the sermon. This was the part he dreaded. Was he to be humiliated in public along with his wife and family and his name read off the altar, the ultimate condemnation in front of his whole community? The whole village was waiting in thrilled anticipation for the sermon. Its possible contents had been the talk of the locality for days before and there was a frisson of excitement in the chapel as the priest mounted the pulpit. It was the moment all Kildangan had been waiting for. Father Ryan was known not to mince his words, this would be a ripper of a sermon and no doubt about it. The priest ponderously ascended the steps to the wooden pulpit, giving even more gravity and excitement for the awaited sermon. The pulpit was a good six foot above his parishioners forcing them to arc their heads to see the priest. He slowly removed his biretta and stared down at the people of Kildangan. It was a dramatic silence preparing them for what was to come. Not a sound was heard from the congregation, even the habitual coughing stopped. Tommy looked up but quickly averted his eyes in case the priest was staring at him and others would notice this.

"Dearly beloved people of Kildangan," roared the priest. "We thank God and his holy Mother this day that the people of Ireland, the land of Saint Patrick, Saint Colmcille and our own St Brigid of Kildare, has been delivered from a Godless conspiracy, hatched abroad and nurtured at home by those who would lead our young men down the garden path to lawbreaking and eternal damnation.

Today all over Ireland the Lord Bishops of the land have issued a Lenten Pastoral condemning the Fenian uprising of the last week as wicked and sinful and I will read it to you presently. I stand before you today to tell you that anyone involved in this conspiracy from our peaceful and prosperous parish, ruled over by so benevolent a landlord of the true faith, will incur the wrath of God, yes, the dreadful wrath of God".

At this he slapped pulpit to emphasise the importance of his pronouncement and then he went silent for a moment so that the congregation could digest his words. In a lower voice he continued "Very little blood has been shed, and we thank divine providence for that and for the work of the constabulary in stamping out the flames of revolt against our lawful rulers before they got out of hand"

Tommy looked at his father who looked back but didn't betray any hint of how he felt about the priest's tirade.

"The conspiracy was opposed to human and divine law, it is a movement foolish in the extreme and because foolish and without any chance of success it was even more sinful in the eyes of heaven.

It was utterly senseless, mischievous and indeed calculated to cause bloodshed and hardship. If it had succeeded it would have driven the wealthy from our shores, the captains of industry from our cities and the landowners from our countryside. Its success, God forbid, would have increased the evils of absenteeism by driving out our land-owning class. It would have paralysed trade and diminished employment. In short it would have brought misery and poverty to our fair land.

Besides being a mortal sin to take arms against our lawful authorities there is the question of membership of a seditious and secret organisation.

Membership of the Fenian conspiracy is based on a secret oath.

This is contrary to the laws of God and of our mother the church and has been condemned by the Holy Father, Pope Pius IX. All who have been contaminated by this oath must confess it as a grievous sin in confession and God's infinite mercy will be forthcoming. Those who do not must face hellfire for eternity if they die with this sin on their souls, yes, my dear people, hellfire for all eternity.

Think about that, my dear people, the flames of hell licking your body from head to toe for all eternity in the company of the devil and all the evil ones from the start of time"

"There goes Jimmy Dunne. His arse roasted for eternity" thought Tommy, "he'll never confess it as a sin."

A smile came to his lips, then his face froze again, he was sure people were looking at him for his reaction and he must not give them cause for gossip.

"It was foolish in the extreme to think that a group of poorly armed, poorly led and uneducated men could wrest this country from England and to lead young men into this belief was wicked.

Many of these young men, so led, are guilty of foolishness and sin themselves but their leaders and agitators are guilty of far greater sins.

It is better for a millstone to be tied around their necks and they be cast into eternal darkness than to give scandal to the young ones.

That's what it says about their likes in the Bible, the word of God himself"

Now he raised his voice for emphasis. "Hell is not hot enough for them that lead the young people astray. It is for the fathers and mothers of this parish to ensure that no-one from around here endangers his mortal body or far more important his eternal soul into the hands of this sinful conspiracy. It is a dreadful responsibility placed on the shoulders of the parents of this parish. Not only the wellbeing of your sons here on earth but their eternal life depends on it.

Remember, my dear people that there is no reprieve from hell. All men and women are sinners since the creation of the world, except of course, the Blessed Virgin Mary and we will all spend time in purgatory to atone for our sins, but our time there is finite and can be mitigated by the prayers and good deeds of the faithful. But there is no such thing as a reprieve from hell, it is eternal suffering and pain and the pain of burning at that. We all know the pain of burning. It is the greatest pain that can be inflicted.

Let those who contemplate joining the Fenian conspiracy contemplate this"

Charles More O'Ferrall nodded in agreement. Those government idiots in Dublin Castle really hadn't a clue. They thought coercion and repression by the police force and soldiers would pacify Ireland. What a confederacy of fools! All that was needed in Ireland was to have the priests on your side, that would ensure a peace loving and law abiding country. That had always been his policy. Fr. Ryan was a wonder! How clever of him to place the responsibility for law and order on the parents, that would involve the whole parish in keeping the peace. He had the congregation eating out of the palm of his hand. They were taking in every word he said. They would remember and talk about this sermon for the rest of their lives and what's more important, act on it. Thomas Brennan would learn his lesson and his parents would ensure that he did. The words rang in Tommy's ears, he hadn't really considered it in this light at all. Maybe there was something in what the priest had said.

When Fr Ryan left the pulpit the silence of the congregation continued, everyone felt guilty and subdued even those who had no hand, act of part in the rising, thinking that maybe they too were guilty in some way. Thank God he had made confession the night before, Tommy thought, he would have stood out like a sore thumb if he hadn't been able to receive Communion, later on in the Mass. Then people would know he had an unconfessed sin on his soul. When the Communion was given out, he was able to march up with his wife, mother and father and partake. He didn't look around but he could feel Mr More O'Ferrall's eyes burning into his back. Indeed he rightly thought everyone's eyes were on him. When he opened his mouth to receive the consecrated bread his eyes looked straight into Fr Ryan's. He felt sure the priest knew his guilty secret even though it was another priest to whom he confessed the previous night. He had to gulp to swallow the bread, so dry his mouth had become from nervousness, but he didn't flinch.

Back in their house the Brennans sat down to a simple Lenten breakfast of bread, butter and tea. The adults were joined by James and Nicholas, the children of the house, they sat silently at the end of the table. Children were expected to be seen and not heard. No mention had been made of the priest's sermon till then. Old Willy buttered a slice of bread and before he ate it said "In my day the leaders of the people made up their own minds and the priests followed them, it seems to be the other way round nowadays."

"What do you mean?" asked his son, relieved that the subject was now to be discussed at last. "In the old days, Daniel O'Connell, God rest his soul, got us the right to have members in parliament and Catholic Emancipation and the priests followed him, I don't remember them getting us anything, but now they seem to rule the roost."

"Don't talk like that in front of the child after all he's been through, didn't you hear what the priest said?" declared his wife as she glared at him. "How often have I told you before, woman, he's not a child?" said Willy "and anyway, we can make up our own minds around here, we don't have to be dictated to from the pulpit."

Now it was Julia's turn to chip in. "No respectable family would go against the priests, it's the priests who lead the people and we must follow. The good old days, as you call them were full of wickedness and ignorance. There was a lot of paganism in this country before the Famine" she said mildly but with great firmness.
There was a shocked silence around the table, Julia had

developed a quiet but effective way of dropping bombshells and laying down the law. None of them had ever heard Julia express an opinion so strongly before and in such a tone as didn't allow contradiction and for her to go against her father-in-law was something new in the house.

"So that's it" said Willy "the country is to be run by the priests from now on?" "Maybe they would make a better fist of it than those who have gone before" said his wife. Now it was the two women against Willy. This had never happened before. He looked at Tommy for support but none was forthcoming. Tommy was in shocked silence "How can a priest know what's best for the people, they don't even know what it is to have a family or be with a woman?" "You can cut out that dirty talk Willy Brennan, the priests are the people of God, now eat your breakfast, I've had enough of this type of chatter, its bad luck to speak disrespectfully about the clergy." "I can see it all clearly now" said Willy bitterly. "The country will be run by priests and women, well if that's the case then God help Ireland"

When his prediction drew no response he raised his voice. "God damn it women, can we not talk about things anymore?" and even as he said this he regretted it, he had never spoken crossly in front his daughter-in-law before, but after that he shut up, signalling an end to the conversation and his defeat and submission to the new order.

Tommy had turned beetroot red with embarrassment for his father, his mother, his wife and children, believing that this whole altercation was his fault.

Everything was his fault, and now his family were at one another's throats in a way that had never happened before.
"I won't have nothing to do with the Fenians no more" he said. The rest of the meagre breakfast was consumed in silence.

Chapter 11

The Blackbird of Sweet Avondale

By the bright bay of Dublin, while carelessly strolling,
I sat myself down by a clear crystal shade,
Reclined on the beach while the wild waves were rolling,
In sorrow condoling I spied a fair maid.

Her hopes changed to mourning that once were so glorious.
I sat in amazement to hear her sad tale.
Her heartstrings burst forth in wild accents deploring,
Saying "Where is my blackbird of sweet Avondale?

Through the counties of Wicklow, Kerry, Cork and Tipperary,
The praises of Ireland my blackbird did sing,
But woe to the hour, with heart light and airy,
That heaved from my arms to Dublin took wing.

All the birds in the forest, their notes there to cheer me
Not even the song of the sweet nightingale,
Her notes so encharmning fills my heart with alarm,
Since I lost my blackbird of sweet Avondale.

Oh the Peelers waylaid him, in hopes to ensnare him,
While I here in sorrow his absence bewail
It grieves me to think that the walls of Kilmainham

Surrounds my poor blackbird of sweet Avondale.

Oh, Erin, my country, awake from your slumbers
And bring back my Blackbird, so dear onto me
And let everyone see, by the strength of your numbers
That we, as a nation, would wish to be free"

A ballad commemorating the jailing of Charles Stewart Parnell.
"The uncrowned King of Ireland" in Kilmainhan Jail in 1882.

Sunday 28th June 1891.

It was a balmy Sunday's night at the end of June that he would never forget it the longest day he lived and not for any good reason. All his Sunday jobs were done around the house and the stock looked after. Julia sat beside the fire knitting and darning to her heart's content. Her hair was now grey and tied up in a bun the way his mother's had been but she had lost her slim figure. She was now a matronly and stout woman as befitting her status a respectable tenant farmer's wife. It seemed as if she had turned into her mother-in-law in appearance at least. Their eldest son James had repaired to the Public House where he was almost a fixture. The old cat and the Collie dog Shep lay asleep at her feet or pretending to be so that they wouldn't be disturbed. Her daughters Alice and Annie sat chatting to their mother while he sat opposite his wife at the other side of the fire. He was smoking his pipe and thinking about the week ahead and fretting about the fate of his great leader Charles Stewart Parnell. He was in a bit of trouble, having married a divorcee; Catherine O'Shea, three days previously.

Worse still, in his eyes anyway, he had been cited in Mrs O'Shea's divorce case as co-respondent which meant that he had been carrying on with her while she was still married to Captain O'Shea.

O'Shea was a right scoundrel, everyone knew that, but Parnell had promoted him as the Irish Party candidate in Galway and he was elected as a Member of Parliament even though he wasn't even a supporter of Home Rule. That stank to high heaven, it seemed to all that he had been given the seat so that he would turn a blind eye to the Leader's relationship with his wife. Now Parnell had refused to resign as leader of the Irish Parliamentary Party and the English Liberal Party under Prime Minister Gladstone had refused to progress the Home Rule Bill for Ireland while the Irish Party was led by an adulterer. They were very strict about things like that, and most of the Irish MPs felt the same. All the progress that the Irish had made towards Home Rule, a parliament for themselves in Dublin and the right to run their own affairs was now in danger but Parnell refused to step aside. He was a stubborn man, everyone knew that but surely he could see how dangerous the situation was and do the right thing?

There was a smouldering fire in the grate in spite of the high summer that they were enjoying but the fire had never been let go out since the family had lived into that house in Kildangan over a hundred years ago. It would be bad luck to let it out, another piece of old bladder, thought Tommy but his wife was very keen on the old superstitions. These sat very comfortably with her alongside her strict observance of church laws. Not for the first time Tommy thought of what a contradiction she was, but she was loyal and kind hearted and had been a good wife for nearly forty years and a loving mother too.

She was also a great manager of money and was responsible for paying the rent on the 15 acres that they proudly possessed, let to them by Mr More O'Ferrall back in the eighties. That was a big step up in life for the Brennans, moving from being yard workers to being tenant farmers, even if their holding was small enough. Tommy wasn't ashamed to admit that they could never have done it without her careful management and planning. Like many tenant farmers' wives, she managed the finances and he knew that when the time came they would be able to buy out their place. That's the way things were going in Ireland and about time too. Many tenant farmers had already bought out their homesteads from their landlords. This arrangement suited him perfectly as he had always liked a quiet life, in his own home especially. She was good at what she did and was a strong willed woman. He let her have her way in most things for the sake of peace. He hated confrontation and especially in his own home but he didn't feel close to her and hadn't done so since the early days of their marriage.

He supposed that many families were like this but he knew he was lucky in so many ways. His parents and grandparents were happy to have enough food on the table and a roof over their heads. Why did he want more?

It looked a lovely homely scene he thought, domestic tranquillity but it wasn't peaceful at all. Himself and Julia were locked in a nasty verbal battle over the Irish Party Leader, Charles Stewart Parnell and his marriage to a divorcee, or maybe it was over religion, he wasn't sure which, maybe both. Politics and religion were all mixed together nowadays. He supposed they always were in Ireland. Every interaction between him and his wife was now barbed and intended to undermine the other. In all fairness though, it wasn't only her, all the women in the house were against him. Jesus, these women were bitter about Mr. Parnell, worse that the men even, far worse in fact and the men were bad enough, at each others throats, up and down the country. Listening to the priests of course, the lot of them. The priests didn't want the Irish to be led by a Protestant, he had always believed that, they wanted a Catholic that they could dictate to, and nobody could dictate to Mr Parnell, not even the priests of his own religion. He liked him for that. But there was more to it than that and he knew it. "She must be a brazen bitch all the same, that Mrs Kitty O'Shea woman, marrying Mr Parnell in the sight of God and her own husband still living" his daughter Alice had spat out, her eyes narrowing with the intensity of her bitter words. "English women have no morals at all." "Sure it wasn't a real marriage anyway" her mother threw in, "wasn't even in a Protestant Church, it was in a Registry Office, sure that's no marriage at all. It's a sin as well."

Charles Stewart Parnell (1846-1891)

He knew that this performance was being put on to ridicule his support for Mr Parnell.

" Even the Protestants wouldn't let the pair of them darken a church doorway, it just shows what they are thought of in their own country" said Annie with spite in her voice. She had been listening in silence hoping that they would get off the subject and move onto something less controversial and surprised herself at the vehemence of her own contribution. This was too much for Tommy who had held his tongue. Now though he knew that he was as much the target of abuse as was was his Leader.

"Annie, Mr Parnell is as Irish as you and me. Why the hell do you think he's called the Blackbird of Sweet Avondale in the ballad. Sure he's from Rathdrum in Wicklow just across the hills, as you know well. His whole family going back the generations are Irish patriots and you know that well too. You should be a bit more Christian in your attitude and if you can't be Christian at least you should stick to the facts not like the other ignoramuses up and down the country. It's a love match, surely you can understand that, maybe they couldn't help themselves? And Alice, her name is Catherine not Kitty" "A love match, what kind of nonsense is that Daddy?" his wife asked. He hated it when she called him "Daddy" and she knew it too. "They're grown people, not much younger than you and me. Carrying on like a pair of beasts out in the fields, a love match indeed and to think that the men of Ireland were taken in by him for so long. I always knew there was something unwholesome, something not quite right about him and as for that woman, well, God will judge her." She looked pointedly at her husband who was now white with anger. He knew this was a dig at him, he had been a great Parnell supporter, travelling far and wide to canvass for his candidates, joining his Land League and becoming the face of the movement in Kildangan. "For your information the man you're talking about, Charles Stewart Parnell who along with Michael Davitt brought landlordism to its knees in Ireland and if it wasn't for them and the movement they led we wouldn't have this house and land. What's more they nearly won freedom for Ireland and our own parliament and they can still do it"

"Well, you know what they say Daddy" said Annie. She was the cheekiest of his daughters and his favourite, "Nearly never bulled a cow" she repeated and Alice giggled with laughter. "Now Annie" said her mother disapprovingly," We'll have none of that farmyard talk in this house. Its bad enough talking about that man and the way he married his trollop"

"Right" Tommy said "I've heard enough. I'm off down to the Crossed Keys, I might find someone down there with a bit of charity in them, you'd think he done it all just to spite ye."

As he closed the half-door behind him he turned when he heard his wife say after him "Maybe he did" and saw his daughters smirk.

What the hell was it in decent people that brought out such venom and in his own family as well?

As he walked down the road, he wished that sometimes he should stand up more to people that he disagreed with, especially in his own family. He always found it easier to think his own thoughts while all around him people were saying things he completely disagreed with. It was more than looking for a quiet life, he knew that. It was a flaw in his character, he should let people know how he felt. When he was silent in front of people who expressed opinions he disagreed with, sometimes they thought he agreed with them because of his silence. Sometimes he didn't even stand up to bad behaviour. His whole life had been like this: he had never been able to connect with anyone. He just seemed to be alone with his own thoughts all the time.

At the start of his marriage he was sure share his ideas and feelings with his wife Julia, but no, that proved to be just the lust of the bed and the mutual advantage of rearing a family and keeping a house. The comfort of family life. He often felt that he was living with a stranger. He thought that he had that connection with Billy Britain in those far off days in the Crimea and maybe he had, but that had never been tested before Billy died and sometimes he doubted if it would have lasted. But Billy was the one he thought about most in his life and he could share his secret thoughts with no one else...not a soul. Of course he was too young and foolish then. They both were. As for his friends in Kildangan, they were just company: small talk and banter. Sometimes he thought he had that connection with Jimmy Dunne especially the time that they both rode out to the Fenian rebellion but he knew in his heart and soul that Jimmy did not have those feelings for him. He was not capable of them. How he envied the old people, his father and the Widow Delaney, even his

mother before her dotage! They chatted, engrossed in one another's ideas and opinions, so respectful and interested in each other. He never had anything like that, just standing there listening, occasionally intervening but all the time feeling like he was an interloper.
At least he was materially comfortable but that was not enough for a full life. He felt that he was missing the most important thing in life.
But that was the way he was since he went to the Crimea and he was not going to change now. He was too old for anything to happen for the better. He would keep quiet for the sake of peace. People would think he was mad if he tried to explain all this to them. A few pints of porter would help anyway. They would calm things down in his own head.

Now as he strode down the road, he never felt so lonely in his whole life. It was only a mile's walk down to the Crossed Keys Public House and he made it in twenty five minutes, taking large strides to get some distance from the dark thoughts in his own head and to cool himself down after the character assassination he had heard in his own house. He had calmed considerably by the time he reached his destination. Inside the Public House he greeted the landlord, Jimmy Kennedy, a comrade of his from the old Crimean days. "Great weather we're having, Jimmy, hope it continues." "With the help of God" Jimmy replied pouring Tommy a pint of creamy porter even before he had put in an order. The long counter was lined with men, some standing, some seated on high stools while others sat by the window, most were drinking the black porter with the creamy head, other more seasoned drinkers had tumblers of whiskey in front of them, which they called chasers to accompany their pints. There was a great chatty atmosphere in the room and the air was heavy and aromatic with pipe smoke mixing with the sweet smell of the beer and the dried sweaty smell of men which increased as they warmed up from the heat of the room and the effects of the alcohol. Though it wasn't quite dark yet, the room was lit by the warm glow of the tilly lamp hung from the ceiling. There was a welcoming and warm feeling in here Tommy thought, far from the women and children and the week's work and worries and the dark thoughts inside his head. Immediately he began to relax. He went to join his son James who was propped up at the end of the counter with two cronies laughing and talking away.

"Howya Daddy?" James acknowledged his father.

"I was just telling the boys here about Mr More O'Ferrall's new brood mare The Lady. "Its Mr Dominick's horse" said Tommy. "Since his father died he intends to make a great name for himself as a horse breeder. Sure, it's in his blood. His family were great breeders of horses going back the generations."

"And his mother's family were great breeders of all sorts of livestock too, they supplied horses for the army as far back as Waterloo and before, or so I have been told" dropped in Sean Kinsella, a tall, skinny man who spent most of his time in James's company. "Indeeding they were. God rest her soul" replied Tommy "and sure why don't you give us your recitation about the More O'Ferralls while you're at it?" Sean didn't need a second invitation. He was the local poet, a tall, spare man known for his loud laugh, his great sense of humour and he had an opinion on everything, much of what he turned into verse for the amusement of the locals and himself. He went from fair to fair all over south Kildare and Queen's County selling penny broadsheets of ballads, most of his own composing. A few of the locals said that it was he who wrote "The blackbird of sweet Avondale", the ballad about Parnell and he did nothing to dispel the rumour though Tommy had his doubts. In fact Jimmy Dunne had christened him "The crow of Kildangan" as he had a woeful singing voice.

"It was in November I'll always remember
The day of the month and the date of the year
It was in Kildangan the bells I heard ringin'
And to meet a foxhunt a course I did steal

The bells caused a humming, I just heard them coming
Away in the distance the noise of the hounds
And I being elevated, I patiently waited
Till the huntsmen and dogs had entered the grounds

That famed More O'Ferrall whose
deeds they are glorious
And his gracious lady till this latter day
For breeding such foxes, great horses and oxes
For feeding and breeding he still holds the sway"

As Sean's recitation died down the men around muttered "Good on you Seanie" and looked into their pints. They had heard it all a hundred times before or at least it felt like that. They were less than grateful to

Tommy for giving the village poet another opportunity to recite, not that he needed much of an invitation. At least he didn't inflict "The blackbird of sweet Avondale" on them but this was not a night to bring up the issue of Parnell. Now flushed with the thrill of an audience he turned to James. "And tell me Jimmy " said Sean with a mischievous smile on his face, "Did you ever ride the Lady?" "No indeed I didn't" said James, then quick as a flash he added "but I often rode a beggar woman".

The men burst into loud guffawas and Tommy smiled indulgently at his son and thought what a ticket he was, always with a ready answer and a joke about everything but it was about time he got married and settled down. He was nearly thirty now. He was so unlike himself or Julia, so outgoing, so social and more that a bit wild and reckless. He often thought that his son was a throwback to a previous generation and then he thought sadly of Nicholas in America, he was the son more like himself. He had applied for a land grant in a place called Minnesota, maybe he would become an American farmer, fancy that!

Nicholas had seen clearly that there was no future for himself in Ireland. As the second son, he knew that James would inherit the farm, so quite rightly he headed for the New World: he was never afraid to march to the beat of his own drum. What would it be like in America? Tommy mused, he wouldn't mind being there himself on this night. He had been to the Crimea and that had shaped his life and he thought of it nearly every day. In spite of his loneliness he was content enough in Kildangan, at least he was comfortable, plenty to eat and drink, a nice house and family. But it wasn't enough, he didn't know why but he knew it wasn't. He sometimes longed for the adventure, uncertainty and opportunity that life in a new country would bring. Or maybe a friendship that would mean something to him. But that was for a young man without responsibilities. He was too old now to do anything about it.

James was too fond of the drink too, he often worried about that, it was the ruin of many a good man. Many a reputation was lost on a barstool. It was a terrible thing to have a son that you didn't feel in tune with, it was a curse. He would never admit that to anyone though, not even his wife. It was an unnatural thing.

His daughters were cheeky and high spirited, he liked that, though they were very sharp about Mr. Parnell but yet again he never really felt close to them like most people in his life.

He had made good matches for them with farmer's sons and supplied them with a decent dowry: twenty pounds each. Their husbands could deal with their sharp tongues. God help them! The day of the love match was over but that was the modern world. Well maybe it was still the way for the offspring of poor people but not for farmers' daughters, they had to stick to their own class or they might endanger the ownership of the land which had been so long and hard fought for.

Just then he saw his old friend and comrade Jimmy Dunne, his big frame being supported by the counter.

He hoped he hadn't been there all the time looking at him. He was now the village blacksmith in succession to his father. He had left Kildangan after the Fenian Rising fiasco and gone to Dublin and later to America but had returned as soon as his father died and nobody had bothered him about the Fenians.

He looked every inch the part of a blacksmith: big and burley, with a generous belly now, attached to his already big frame. He must have come in while he was talking to James and his pals. Flushed up with his first pint in ages and in better humour now after his banter with James and Sean Kinsella, Tommy walked over to Jimmy and said "Come on Jimmy, let me buy you a pint." They had fallen out over the Parnell affair. Jimmy had remained with Parnell, whom he called the Chief while Tommy, along with most of the Irish people had supported the Parliamentary Party who had deposed Parnell as their leader. The Irish Parliamentary Party at Westminster was now led by Mr Justin McCarthy, the MP for Longford and Tommy had thrown in his lot in with them.

They would get Home Rule through Parliament with the help if the Liberal Party, sooner or later.

Nevertheless he was now on the same side as the priests for the first time in his life. Maybe he was getting more conservative as he grew older.

But this was no way for two old friends to behave thought Tommy.

Afterall, himself and Jimmy Dunne went back a long way having been comrades in the Crimea and friends for all those years after and indeed since their schooldays.

"Well if it isn't my old friend Crimee Tommy, taking a night off from stabbing The Chief in the back are we?" said Jimmy, half joking half serious, but his words cut Tommy to the quick. "Ah, come on Jimmy, that's no way to for two old timers like ourselves to carry on, have a drink on me." "I don't mind if I do Tommy, I'm sorry about the falling out between us two, remember we were Fenians together when all the country sat on their arses. I'm sorry about what I said just now, it just came out".

The pints arrived and Tommy lifted his. "Here's to you Jimmy Dunne, an honourable man and true." Jimmy sipped his pint in silence. Tommy had expected a return of the compliment. Instead there was an awkward silence. Now a real tension developed between the men as they both understood what this silence meant.

"How's your wife and children?" Tommy asked trying to avoid the issue by changing the subject.
"Divil a bother on them" Jimmy answered, "And yours?" "Fine, fine."
Then Jimmy left down his pint and glared at Tommy in that old familiar way that both knew so well when he was heading for confrontation and trouble.
"I see from the Freeman's Journal that Mr Parnell was married last week. Will you join me in a toast to the happy couple, Tommy Brennan?"
"Indeed I will not Jimmy, that man has let down the whole country with his whoring. No man is entitled to marry another man's wife, especially someone who claims to be the leader of the Irish people."
Immediately he was sorry he said that, it just came out,

he didn't even mean it. Jimmy was now rightly riled and gone red in the face with temper and anger. In a louder voice he declaimed "No, he has not, it's you and your likes that's let down the country, touching the forelock to the priests and the traitors in the Parliamentary Party who won't stand up to the English and support The Chief". "Look Jimmy, I don't want to fall out with you again over this, that's why I came over to talk to you in peace and quiet, come on Jimmy for old times sake let's be civil to one another" said Tommy quietly. He was now aware that there was a hush in the room and that many of the men were looking towards them.

Jimmy turned round and faced them, glaring wildly, then he turned back to Tommy. "Well fuck you then and your seed, breed and generation." Then lifting his glass he shouted "Here's to Mr and Mrs Parnell, long may they prosper."

Jimmy Kennedy was over directly. "Jimmy" he said "I want you to go home now like a good fellow, there's no call for talk like that in a respectable house."

"Come on Jimmy, I'll walk you up the road" offered Tommy.

Jimmy swallowed the remainder of his pint and looked around at the other men in the bar as he prepared to leave. The chatter had stopped all around them. Tommy took his old friend by the arm to link him off the premises. Jimmy turned round with his free arm and boxed Tommy right in the face. Tommy staggered back, knocking over the drinks of the men next to him. "Right, that's it, disturbing the peace, throw him out" commanded Jimmy Kennedy and even as he spoke a

group of fellows including James were manhandling Jimmy Dunne out the door. "And don't bother coming back" he shouted.
" I won't darken the door of this dive the longest day I live" Jimmy Dunne roared back as he was dragged onto the street.
"That's for sure," said Jimmy Kennedy as he poured a whiskey for Tommy who now sat slumped on a chair.

Chapter 12

A thief in the night

Sunday 11th October 1891.

It was usually a great pleasure for Tommy to spend his Sunday mornings pottering around the house. But today his heart was heavy with grief and regret. He cleaned the windows front and back, he polished the knocker on the front door, it was his training as a soldier all those many years ago in the barracks at Naas and those years as a soldier that made him enjoy these jobs of cleaning and polishing so much, he reckoned. The young soldiers were always polishing and shining their kits and guns as he remembered now. Later on he would put the pot of potatoes on the crane for the dinner. In the yard he checked the hen-house so that Mr Fox could not get in when they had all retired for the night. His wife had fed them before she went on her rambles, that was usually her job.

He lovingly examined each of the American turkey chicks that he was rearing for Christmas. Everything he saw filled him with pride and contentment relieving somewhat his dark mood. Julia was off visiting Alice, their eldest daughter in her house in Killeen and wouldn't be back until teatime. Their son James was at late mass and would probably drop into the pub for a few scoops before returning for his dinner. His ould mother had died during the previous winter but, in truth she had been doting for many years, lost in her own world. She had been dead to him for many years, almost since his father had died. So he was completely alone in the house. These precious few hours were much valued by him, no one to question or nag him and time to gather his thoughts and refresh his memories and loose himself in them.

How it had all come on since his father's and grandfather's time! He still had real if vague memories of the one-roomed house he was born in, and had seen it grow to the fine three-roomed house in which he now lived. It was a great thing to own you own house with a little bit of land and to be a tenant farmer like the best of them. No longer a farm labourer for the More O'Ferralls like his father and his father's father before him going back to the mists of time, with no security at all and the ever present fear of being put out on the road at the whim of the landlord.

Sometime in the future his son would buy out the farm like so many in Ireland were doing. Tenant Purchase it was called and it was the way forward for the country and it was the modern way. It would change the country into a nation of freeholders. The government loaned the money to the tenant who bought the farm freehold from the landlord. The money would then be paid back to the government over many years at a low interest rate. It was the way forward. That would be a great achievement, to own your own land, even if the landlord had been as good to his family as the More O'Ferralls had been and the O'Reillys before them.

They had just been farm labourers on the estate but Mr

More O'Ferrall had rented land to them, the few acres around their old homestead. It was a great step-up in life and a mark of special favour. He would be able to hand over his homestead and fields to his son James, lock, stock and barrel when the time came and maybe it wouldn't be too long for he was over fifty years now, born the night of the Big Wind as he was often reminded as if that night had been propitious. As the priest was fond of saying "death comes like a thief in the night and "we know not the day nor the hour"...great lines those, the priests knew how to put the fear of God into their congregation and frighten the bejaysus out of them. There was rent to be paid for the land alright but that did not take away from his tenancy and his right to will it to whoever he wanted, not that he would ever think of letting it go to anyone other than his James, that was his birthright as the eldest son. Nicholas, the next eldest son had great prospects in America where he was for many a year. There was no fear of him. He had no worries about Nicholas, no matter what, he would prosper, he was full of get-up-and-go and a great sense of adventure.

His daughters had all made good matches in the locality and not one of them with child before their wedding day or even interfered with before then; his wife's influence, he thought, not his...virgin brides both of them. There was no visiting the Courtin' Tree for them. The poor old Courtin' Tree, he thought, now as redundant as a cut cat. How things had changed since he was a boy! It wouldn't have been like that in those days. But maybe they were making up for it since, especially Alice, she was a frisky one. Farmers' wives the two of them. Not bad for the granddaughters of a yardman at the More O'Ferrall estate, and they called America, the land of opportunity, it was every bit as good in Ireland in the last twenty years.

They were great men indeed, those that had won from the English government the right of the Irish to buy back their land from the landlords. And what was to become of the country now that they were all fighting and bickering with one another? And poor Mr Parnell, dead at the early age of 45, a man in the prime of his life.

If only he had lived another 10 years he might have restored his reputation and come back to unite the nation and to lead it. Or maybe he was just codding himself, some people would never forgive Parnell for what he had done. The priests never would anyway, they were dead set against him. Now he was cold in an English coffin, travelling from Kingstown Harbour to Dublin City for his burial in Glasnevin Cemetery this very day. There'll be some grief when they paraded his corpse through the City and indeed all along the route, Tommy thought. He couldn't understand how a man of his education had let them all down for an English woman.

He was gentry, though, maybe that explained it, that crowd never had to think about the consequences of their actions. Everyone else had to pick up the pieces even from the time when they were children. He was lost in melancholic thought now and went into the kitchen and lit his pipe. He sat beside the fire. An old man sitting by the fire smoking his pipe: this is what his life had come to: comfort and emptiness, waiting for a son he didn't even like. He would sit there till James got home and see what he thought about the big funeral and if he had any news from the village and what the locals said about it. Nicky, his second son had gone to America five years previously. Jimmy Dunne, the local blacksmith and his old friend from Fenian and Crimean days had arranged the whole thing, he had contacts in America. He had been there himself, for a few years after the Fenian rising. He had a man waiting for Nicholas as soon as he got out of the Immigration Centre at Castle Garden in New York, with a job and a place to stay for him. His own brother also called Nicholas has gone to America in the sixties but after a few letters he had disappeared and he hadn't heard anything from him or about him for 20 years. It was the way with many emigrants. They just disappeared. Maybe he was dead at this stage. He would always be grateful to Jimmy Dunne for what he had done for Nicholas, in spite of recent events.

The old Fenians had stuck together and been great supporters of Mr Parnell and the backbone of his organisation but that was all over now. They had split down the middle in the row over his role in Mrs O'Shea's divorce. He has been cited as co-respondent in the case. This meant that he was named as the one who had committed adultery with her. Then to make matters worse he had married her just six months later.
The last real conversation he had with Jimmy on the subject had ended up in a shouting match in The Crossed Keys public house in the village.

Jimmy had hit him a blow and though he apologised, in a sort of a way afterwards, he knew that Jimmy wasn't really sorry.
It was only a matter of form to please his wife and the locals who didn't like his behaviour.
They would probably never talk to one another again, and all over Mr Parnell and Mrs O'Shea. Jimmy had thought that Mr Parnell would be the first President or Prime Minister of the Irish Republic before the century turned. In fact they both had.
Now where were they all going? Who would lead them now that they had been deserted by the Chief for another man's wife and he dead disgracefully in her arms in the English town of Brighton? Nobody had ever built up the hopes of the Irish so much and then let them down so badly.
Nobody, not in the whole history of the land. Jimmy would off to Dublin for the funeral, no doubt. It was all organised by the Fenians anyway. Why didn't they do something about Mr Parnell's philandering, they must have known what was going on years ago?
Hadn't he put forward her husband Captain O'Shea for the bye-election in Galway in 1886 even though he as hostile to Home Rule as the Conservatives and Unionists, everyone knew that.

Captain O'Shea was as bad as any of the Conservatives or Unionists. The Fenians must have known by then what was going on. It was a disgraceful thing, paying off a husband so that a man could carry on with his wife. But he hated what Mr Tim Healy of the Parliamentary Party had said of her, though it now rang in his ears.

He had said that she was a convicted British prostitute. That was going too far, there was no need for language like that, it was a lie anyway.

Mrs O'Shea was a woman of independent means. It was a horrible thing to say about any woman, it made him feel some sympathy for her. Mr. Healy was a bitter Corkman and hated Mr Parnell with an intensity it was hard to understand. Thank God it was at a political meeting in Kilkenny during the bye-election last year and there were no women present to hear such language and such an accusation.

No, it was Mr Parnell's own fault, not the unfortunate woman's. All the same, he supposed that she was no lady. What respectable married woman would carry on like that, leaving her husband for another man, and as for him, wasn't Ireland and the world over full of suitable matches for a gentleman of his standing and he went and picked another man's wife? There must have been hundreds of Irish women who would give their left hand to marry him. He could even have made political capital out of it by marrying a Catholic lady. Was it any wonder that the priests and his own Parliamentary Party and indeed the people of Ireland had turned against him?

He couldn't blame the English Liberal Party for refusing to progress the Home Rule Bill while he remained the Leader of the Irish Parliamentary Party. They were very strict about things like that too, everyone knew that.

What a fine leader Mr Parnell had been before all this

trouble had started though. He remembered his imposing larger-than-life presence, his piercing eyes, his bushy, luxurious beard and his commanding voice. A fine figure of a man and what an orator!

He had been a king alright: the uncrowned King of Ireland, ironically it was that scamp Tim Healy who christened him that. No nickname was ever so apt.

As he sucked on his pipe the tears started to flow, down his face and into his grey beard. He had found that in the last year he was much inclined to do this. As a young man he had never cried, not even when his two young sons or his own father or mother were buried, though he had felt like it. Or even when Billy Britain had died in the Crimea, but then he thought, maybe he did then: in those days he was a young man and full of emotion, he just didn't remember now.

Maybe it was part of being old, this crying, he was reverting to childhood like an old woman who was doting, like his own mother had been. Or maybe it was that at the end of his life he found it all to be such a disappointment. He was so much better off than his father had been and he was surrounded by his family and homestead. But it wasn't enough and he couldn't figure out why. If a man reached sixty in health and comfort, he couldn't complain and he was nearly there. Maybe prosperity had spoiled him. His father's generation didn't have such feelings. They were happy to have a warm bed and enough to eat. Sixty was a long number of years to be in this earth. Maybe it was long enough for him. The priests did a lot of talking about death these days, or maybe it was just the part he heard. Maybe they had always done so and he just hadn't paid attention.

Just then he heard the latch lift on the front door and his son James strutted into the house. He hung his topcoat on the peg beside the door before he strode up to the fire where his father sat silently surrounded by a haze of pipe smoke.

"Have you got the spuds on?" he said gruffly. Then looking at his father and his tear streaked face, he asked "What's the matter with you Daddy?"

"I was just thinking of poor Mr Parnell and all that's happened in the past year. Don't mind me. Is there any news from the village, what's everyone saying?"

"There's a crowd gone up to Dublin for the funeral alright, led of course by that great hero Jimmy Dunne. A crowd of wasters if you ask me. There'll be no work done in Dublin City for a week. That crowd will hit the public houses after the funeral or maybe before and won't leave till their money's run out. I didn't think that you of all people would be crying for that man after the way he has brought shame on all of Ireland."

"I know, I know" his father said softly "but I can't help remembering how great a leader he was in the eighties. The Freeman's Journal called him "The Uncrowned King of Ireland" and we all believed it. He brought the whole country with him, James. There wasn't one man who didn't follow him barring the Orangemen and a few landlords and bigots. He was a great leader back then. I don't know what got into him. What's to become of the country now? Pull up a chair and warm yourself".

James went over to his topcoat and removed his pipe but didn't say a word for awhile, just thinking of how foolish the old people were.

Still he supposed they had been taken in by that horny old codger of a Parnell, you'd think they would be happy now they had their own farms after all they had been through.

He pulled a chair from the kitchen table and sat opposite his father. He lit his pipe before he said anything.

"Sure aren't there great men in the Parliamentary Party, Daddy, men without a stain on their character, men like Mr Healy or Mr Justin McCarthy or Michael Davitt himself who did more to win the land from the landlords than Parnell ever did?"

His father looked into the fire. "There's not a one of them a match for the Chief, didn't he even have the English Prime Minister Gladstone eating out of his hand and he holding the balance of power in Westminster between the Liberals and Conservatives. He was able to control the House of Commons. Don't forget he won 86 seats for the Irish Party at the 1885 General Election. 86 seats, just imagine that! Who could ever do that again? The others can't unite the Irish people, they're not in the same league as Mr. Parnell at all. They're only good at fighting among themselves, the Liberals will run rings around them and the Conservatives will ignore them. There's not a one of them a patch on Parnell.

His son looked at him in wonder. "I can't believe I'm hearing this from you of all people, after all you said to me about Parnell and his trollop in this very house. Control the House of Commons? That man couldn't control his own mickey."

"You're right I suppose" his father replied resignedly, "but I can't help feeling sorry all the same, he could have got freedom for Ireland at last, he was so near, another General Election and the Liberals and Gladstone would have been back in and we would have gotten Home Rule. O'Connell must be turning in his grave. He never had a chance like that. He was the greater man of the two. Ireland was a nation of beggars before O'Connell. He left the country much better off after him. But he was no saint either, Jimmy. They used to say that you couldn't throw a stone over a poorhouse wall without hitting one of his bastards." "I never heard that" his son said. "Its true enough" his father said "we used to laugh at those stories years ago but it was different for Parnell. I suppose it's because he was so brazen about it, marrying that woman and parading her before the world"

"At least the others didn't do it in public, belittling the whole Irish nation. Its one thing to do it in private but Parnell flaunted his carry-on in front of the whole world, at least O'Connell had the decency to keep it quiet" said James. "You mean if he kept it secret and made her his mistress it would have been alright? That's hypocrisy James" "I don't understand you Daddy, you're as much against him as me but now you are defending him"

"Did the priest say anything about it at Mass?"

"Divil a bit, I suppose he was too ashamed to bring up the subject today of all days and that man's funeral taking place in Dublin in a few hours. It wouldn't be right to mention it today.

A priest of all people would never speak ill of the dead. The times have changed Daddy, people are better read now and won't put up with such behaviour from someone who puts himself ahead of everyone as leader of the country.

Its no harm in the long run, how could we ever have a man like that running the country?"

Tommy nodded his head. It was true what his son had said, times had changed. When he was James' age he was out with a gun chasing the dream of an independent Ireland. Now people were more worried about buying their farms, the price of livestock and having something to leave their children.

"No man has a right to set a boundary to the march of a nation" Parnell had said that, but when it applied to himself he couldn't seem to accept it and act on his own words.

The country had come on so much since he was a child in the forties and fifties. Who could tell what it would be like in another 50 or 100 years? In the old days, in his father's and grandfather's time, the people had nothing to lose, because they owned nothing except their own children, not like nowadays. Now they had their own land. That was the biggest change ever: families living in their own homesteads and free to pass them on the next generations and a future for themselves and their children, they were more learned too, all the children went to school nowadays.

Maybe his son was right, maybe the country had grown up.

"The spuds must be nearly done" he said moving from his chair.

II. September 16th 1899

It had been drizzling rain all morning and Tommy had stood at the window for what seemed like hours just looking out and hoping for a break in the weather. He had his topcoat on and his head covered, he hated being stuck in like this and work to be done. The gentle autumn rain pattered on the thatch making a soothing sound that served as a backdrop to Tommy's daydreaming. Out in the yard he watched as it ran down the cowhouse roof and was collected in the wooden barrel at the end of the sheds. Beyond the outhouses he could see the fields misted and shrouded in the rain. It was a pleasant sight, all of it his own little kingdom he thought. All the same he was aching to get out and do some work. He had been feeling very tired and a bit sad for no specific reason all week other than the usual of looking and talking to people he had no interest in.

"Will you come away from the window and sit down by the fire, like a good man, you'll get no work done today" his wife chided him as she busily went about her chores. She seemed happy enough thought Tommy. She was a good woman but she had no capacity for feeling things outside of her own immediate surrounds. She was kneading dough on the kitchen table and humming away to herself. James was still in bed even though it must be passed ten in the morning; that was his way. He was a lazy boy, happy as Larry so long as his belly was full.
But Tommy wouldn't move.

Now he was thinking about an autumn day like this one, in the Crimea many years ago and Julia's voice sounded very far away. He could see Billy Britain's face as clearly as if he was there beside him and then his father's face and Mrs Delaney the old widow woman midwife and the beautiful Susan O'Reilly on her wedding day. Then his dear mother Catherine snuggling him against her voluminous skirts that smelled uniquely of her. So many dead people but he could see them all clearly now, it had been a good life, so many decent people.

He had loved them all and they had shown him great respect.

Presently he took off his topcoat and hat. He moved slowly to the fire and sat down in his armchair. As he stared into the embers, all the people from the past crowded round him but he kept his eyes open as he stared into the flames. As his eyes burned and watered he saw them all: his Daddy and Mammy waiting for him as he came home from school, the poor beggars walking the roads during the famine time: the way he wasn't allowed talk to them or even go near them, in case he caught one of their diseases.

Then the Crimea and the great ship he travelled on and of course Billy Britain, funny how he had missed him all his life, he didn't know why but it didn't matter now. Billy would have been an old man just like himself or more likely than not, dead by now one way or another. Billy was not the type of man who would grow old. He was too adventurous, too reckless. His youthful bravado would have looked foolish even in middle age. And then Jimmy Dunne, he had never gotten over the falling out they had over Parnell. They had been such great friends, travelling all over Leinster and up to Dublin county to take part in the Fenian rising and then the row in the pub over Parnell. Stupid how people fell out over politics, they had been comrades in arms and now they barely acknowledged one another when they passed in the village. He reckoned that their friendship had been one-sided and shallow if it had disappeared over politics. He had stupidly thought at one time that Jimmy could replace Billy in his life. All gone, all alone now in the bosom his family. Funny how one could be surrounded by people who loved you and still feel alone.

He felt his muscles sink into the armchair as if they were becoming detached from his bones.
Now he felt he couldn't stand up even if he tried though he could still see things in his mind's eye. He didn't want to stand up anymore anyway. He felt his heart thump in his chest and a pain shoot through his left arm. So this was it, he thought, he had heard of these symptoms many times before. He stared as if mesmerised into the fire, he could feel his eyes watering as the tears ran down his cheeks. But his mind was still racing. He fancied that he could see the white walls of Sevastopol in the fire and Nicholas his son. Then Mr More O'Ferrall and the renting of his fifteen acres, what an achievement! His children and his children's children would always remember him for that, no man could have done more for his family.
Or maybe they wouldn't remember at all; just take it all for granted the way James did. He didn't care anyway.

He was weary of it all, so weary.
Then he heard Julia as she said loudly with panic in her voice "Daddy are you alright. Say something?" She ran back to the door and got his topcoat and tucked it round him in the armchair. Then she bent over him and whispered the Our Father into his ear but by then Tommy had slipped into oblivion.

The end.

Made in the USA
Middletown, DE
10 December 2024

66451885R00161